JB SCHROEDER

# dreaming of forever with you

Love That Lasts

BOOK 3

Two Feet
Press

11923 NE Sumner St., Ste 843916
Portland, Oregon 97220



Cover art credits go to AndrewLozovyi and NazArtVector via
depositphotos

Print Edition 1.0
ISBN-13: 978-1-943561-21-6

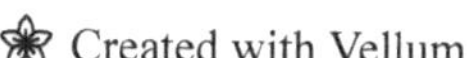 Created with Vellum

*To Derek*

*~*

*Your passion and focus inspire me.*
*To 2052 and beyond.*

# A NOTE ABOUT THIS STORY

At some point around my fifth or sixth book, I realized it was far easier to keep track of a story timeline if I followed a real calendar.

At the end of *Second Chance Love Affair*, Jonah visits Vine to commiserate with Jeremy: a woman is ripping his building out from under him—a gorgeous woman he has history with and desperately wants. That was the setup for *Dreaming of Forever with You*, which meant it, too, needed to follow the 2019-to-2020 calendar.

Of course, by the time Darcy and Jeremy's True Springs wedding occurs in this book, the real 2020 world had already come face to face with the COVID-19 pandemic. The bulk of this story, in fact, was written during our own New Jersey isolation orders.

I'm penning this note on Day 23 of isolation, when I'm just about to write those wedding scenes, so I woke up thinking about the timing. I'm luckier than most. So far, I'm still working the day job from home, my family and friends are still safe, and we still have enough to eat—and yes, enough toilet paper, too.

I considered having my characters deal with real life—Rita having to postpone her big trip and close the diner, Jonah and Kalpani being forced to stay apart—or together—for weeks or months, no one able to grasp hands or kiss or visit—but I prefer for my books to provide an escape. Some realism—real emotions, real struggles, but ones that are surmountable, ones that love and the right partner might just aid in fixing.

Right now, in real life, many will not be able to escape this nightmare at all, their lives changed forever. I'm as scared and stressed as the next person, aware that every-thing could change in an instant. If I were writing one of my darker romantic suspense novels? I'm not sure I could even put words on the screen. For my kids and for my sanity, I have to keep some balance. Nothing too dark, not too much news, not too much reality.

I've always gravitated to romance novels as an escape, and writing lighthearted ones is no different. This story has provided me some relief with which I could block out the real world for hours. I pray, dear readers, that you escape, too—both in books and from reality.

So, yes, I'm letting Kalpani and Jonah skip real life. And, of course, they are guaranteed a happy ending, too.


XOXO,

JB

**1**
———

The bell above the Print & Ship's door wasn't enough to pull Jonah Walker's attention from his creation on the oversized computer screen, but the lilt of Indian voices made his head jolt up.

It wasn't Sohel, of course. The old man had died just a week and a half ago, but the funeral hadn't been held yet, so it was hard to even believe he was truly gone. Sohel's presence in this shop had been such a constant over the years, and his influence on Jonah had been nearly as strong as that of his own father. Jonah wavered between denial and missing Sohel like hell. It didn't help that Jonah had lost his father less than a year ago and had barely come to terms with that.

These visitors were a man and a woman. Sohel's shop —now Jonah's—was a full-service print shop and shipping outlet. Sohel, with Jonah's help in his later years, had done it all: from scanning documents to designing business cards, from xeroxing copies to printing large-scale banners, from selling packing tape to shipping internationally. With all the recent changes in technology, some of their services were rarely sought out these days, while others would likely always be needed. More and more lately, however, it was common for folks to poke their heads in to ask about the art in the window.

This young, well-dressed couple wasn't even looking at Jonah, however.

Their backs were to him and they were chatting among themselves in what Jonah thought of as Inglish—half Indian and half English. What *were* they doing? Inspecting the ceiling and the walls?

Jonah stood and approached the counter before clearing his throat. "Can I help you?"

The couple turned and—

*Whoa.* Jonah's heart thumped hard even as his body tensed. Because standing in front of him was the woman he'd kissed—like, a whole year ago—and hadn't been able to get out of his mind since.

"Jonah, isn't it?"

*Excellent.* She apparently hadn't suffered the same fate, if she wasn't even sure of his name.

He nodded. "Kalpani," he said, trying to avoid any inflection. He'd loved the way her name rolled off his lips. He'd said it over and over again that night. As he kissed her neck, her jaw, her lips… She'd been dressed in a traditional sari then, whereas now she wore skinny black pants, a hot-pink blouse, short-heeled boots, and a tailored, nubby winter coat. She was no less gorgeous.

Jonah came around the counter and approached them. "I'm sorry about Sohel. I understand the funeral is Friday."

"Thanks. Condolences to you as well." Her dark eyes

darted away. "Yes. And there's a luncheon after at the community center."

The very same community center they'd snuck out back of to make out like teenagers and talk until morning. Hadn't mattered that he was twenty-seven—he'd just wanted to get the long-haired, petite beauty with the mischievous eyes and kissable lips alone.

"This is my cousin, Ajay," Kalpani said.

Ajay nodded, but his smile was fake. He pulled a business card from the back pocket of his fitted slacks and extended it to Jonah with two fingers, then he rocked back on his shiny shoes and shoved his thumbs in his pockets.

Jonah looked at the card. Dude was a real estate agent. *Nice.* Jonah had just finally come into owning something —the first thing ever, and it just happened to be a prime piece of property in the 'burgh's hopping Strip District— and already the vultures were circling.

"I'm not interested in selling," Jonah said, and extended the card back to Ajay.

His eyebrows rose, but Kalpani's mouth dropped open. She said, "Excuse me?"

Ajay hadn't taken the card, so Jonah let it fall to the floor. He crossed his arms. "You heard me."

"But what do you mean?" she said.

"Just what I said. I'm not selling. So you and your cousin can stop eyeballing my building and go find some other listing and client to harass."

If possible, Kalpani's jaw dropped further.

Ajay gave him a placating smile. "I think there's been a misunderstanding. This building is for sale. I'm representing it—"

*What the fuck?* "Like hell—"

"Wait," Kalpani said, throwing a hand out. "Didn't Uncle Sohel's lawyer contact you?"

Kalpani wasn't directly related to Sohel, but all the elder men in her culture were referred to as uncles by the younger generations, related or not. Even as Jonah's mind darted through the labyrinth of Sohel's network of family and friends, a sinking feeling settled in his gut.

"No. Sohel's not even buried yet, remember?" Jonah uncrossed his arms—subconsciously needing them free, bracing for a fight.

Kalpani shut her eyes and shook her head. She sucked in a deep breath and pinned him with a hard, heated look— an entirely different kind of heat than she'd graced him with last year, when her hands had slid into his hair and she'd pulled his head down for a mind-melting lip-lock.

"Uncle Sohel's estate—in its entirety—was left to his family."

Jonah blinked rapidly as if moving his eyelids would make sense of that statement. "No," he said. "No, he left the shop to me."

She shook her head. "That's simply untrue."

"He showed me the will," Jonah said, probably too loud.

"Look," Kalpani said, her nostrils flaring, "I don't know what you are trying to pull, but you can cut the bull-shit right now. The Gupta family now owns this property, they've asked Ajay to sell it, and I will be buying it. Period."

"Get out," Jonah said.

The cousins stared at him.

"Get. Out." Jonah lunged forward, and finally the duo

burst into action, spinning away from him. Ajay put his arm around Kalpani as if to protect her as they hustled for the door.

The bell jangled happily even though they yanked the door hard. The sounds of pedestrian traffic flowed in as it swung shut ever so slowly.

Then Jonah was left with only the sounds of his own ragged breathing. Worse was the growing fear that despite all his hard work, dedication, and promises made, he'd just lost everything.

———

Kalpani hit the street nearly in shock. What she was most surprised about, however, she didn't even know.

"Is Jonah trying to pull a fast one? Or is it possible that Uncle Sohel's lawyer hasn't even been in contact with him?"

Ajay shrugged. "He's a nobody, so maybe—"

"To you, but he and Sohel were close. He's obviously still running the Print & Ship. And apparently, he believes he owns the place."

"There's no way."

"He says Sohel showed him the will." She threw her hands up. "There better not be some alternate will out there."

"There isn't. Lawyers keep a very tight leash on these things."

Kalpani narrowed her eyes. Ajay had always been a bit of a know-it-all, and yet, like her, he hadn't gone the Ivy League college route in order to make his single-minded

Indian parents proud. She and Ajay had wanting to buck the traditional and make their own way in common. "And you and your supposedly highest-grossing office are supposed to be topnotch. How is it that you haven't been down here to preview this place and save me from that scene?"

"Because as our friend in there said, Sohel hasn't been gone that long, and *you* were all fired up to get first dibs on the place." He made a face at her—and she suddenly realized that working with someone you'd known since you were in diapers probably wasn't going to make for a very professional relationship.

Kalpani scowled. "Damn straight I was. And I still am." She just never imagined that the shop hadn't been closed.

"You need to fix this," she told him. "Fast. Because it's mine." It had to be, just had to. She *needed* this.

"I'm on it. That asshole will be out on the street in no time."

Kalpani winced. Jonah wasn't an asshole. If Jonah really believed Sohel had left him the building and business—and inexplicably, he seemed to—then he was just reeling and reacting. She felt for him because…well, that really sucked. Throwing them out seemed out of character. She'd believed him to be a nice, laid-back guy.

Heck, it was why she'd let down her guard with him—snuck out back the night of Sohel's seventy-fifth birthday party to kiss and talk and laugh. He was cute and hot and funny—and she'd been insanely attracted to him. He'd been respectful, too. When their kisses and petting turned too hot, he suggested a walk around the neighborhood. And when they returned to the party, they'd gone right back to their spot under a big oak tree, snagging a blanket from her car and talking until the wee hours—long after the party had wrapped up. He'd mentioned he hoped to see her again soon. But she'd simply kissed him one last time and slipped away. She didn't do relationships, so for her, that had to be that.

Ajay had his phone to his ear already.

"Try to be sensitive in your handling of this, okay?" Kalpani said. "Jonah's in a bad spot through no fault of his own."

Ajay rolled his eyes. "I'll be professional. Like always."

Kalpani blew out a breath. She hoped that didn't mean heartless. She didn't want Jonah hurt.

And yet she couldn't let it matter that she'd cherished the hours she and Jonah had spent together. Or that she'd thought of him often, especially when she was in bed at night, alone and needy, remembering the warm look in his eyes, the gravelly sound of his voice, the sexy things he'd said when he'd kissed her.

Sohel's place coming available was an opportunity she couldn't pass up, right along with her friend Darcy's newfound desire to invest in small local businesses. She'd never score a property this ideal for a price this low without her family's connection to the Gupta family. She had planned to save for another couple of years, but this property was worth moving up her timeline and charging full steam ahead. With its prime location and her talent and drive, Xanadu—a name she'd picked years ago—would soon be the most happening salon in Pittsburgh.

It wasn't about fame or fortune. Becoming successfully independent was personal, even essential—the only way she knew to ensure that she'd never fall into a trap like so many women of her culture. And becoming more pressing all the time: she'd be able to help her best friend—far more than she was able to help now.

There was no way she could let a brown-haired, green-eyed, broad-chested, jeans-wearing hottie get in her way.

**2**

———

The phone rang in the print shop, and when Jonah answered, a voice said, "Mr. Jonah Walker? This is Vyas Nath with Anders, Nath, and Jindal. I represent the estate of Sohel Gupta."

*What a surprise.* Jonah gritted his teeth. Not even a few hours after Kalpani and her cousin had left.

Jonah put the attorney on hold. He needed to finish shipping Mrs. Wojtiski's monthly care package to her granddaughter, who was serving in the Marines overseas. He used triple bubble wrap for the flaky Polish cookies, just like always, and today he wrapped them extra slow.

Jonah asked, "You think she shares these *kolaczkis* with her team or just hoards them?"

"A little of both, I imagine." Mrs. Wojtiski smiled as she counted out change.

"I'm sending some safe wishes along with this, Mrs. W," Jonah told her. He'd known the Wojtiskis forever. They'd been regular customers at his parents' diner, The Wanderlust, since before he was born.

"You and me both," she said, wrapping her official Steelers scarf around her neck. "You doing all right here without Sohel?"

Jonah couldn't help a sigh. "It's surreal."

She nodded. "I know. I felt the same when I came through that door. But he'd be glad to know you're keeping the doors open, Jonah."

Jonah nodded, but a heavy cloud of worry hung over him as he returned to the phone.

"All right, Mr. Nath. I'm free to talk now," he told the attorney.

"I understand there's been a misunderstanding about Sohel's intentions, and I apologize for not contacting you sooner," Nath said. "My clerk is on medical leave, so we're a little scattered around here."

Jonah wished he'd just cut to the chase—and then immediately wished he hadn't.

"Mr. Walker, the deceased did not specify that any one portion of his assets be handled individually. The will leaves his estate in its entirety to his brother. You have no claim to the building or the business. In fact, if you are still running the business, you should stop."

"But Sohel showed me the new will he'd had drawn up," Jonah said. "After his heart attack. He asked me if I'd be willing to stay on and take over when he died. He was worried about his customers and didn't want to let them down." Jonah thought of Mrs. Wojtiski and all the other customers who'd been so loyal over the years. His chest felt tight and his temples throbbed. "I told him that it was too much—for him to leave me his business—but he insisted."

Jonah had thought it was an awfully extravagant,

overly generous gesture, but the fact was that Sohel had lost his wife long ago and had no children. Jonah had worked for Sohel so long that they considered each other family.

"You are the only one I trust to take care of everybody like I would," Sohel had said. "I would have had to close up my establishment long ago if it wasn't for you. Jonah, you have earned this." And he swept his gnarled hand through the room—as proud of his narrow shop as if it was a palace.

"Still, Sohel, people just don't hand over buildings and businesses like they're a favorite piece of jewelry or furniture."

"I am your boss, so you don't argue with me," Sohel said, and took the sheaf of papers into the back room. "This is what I want." His accent had deepened with his conviction, and Jonah had known to drop it.

After Sohel had read through the document and declared himself satisfied, he'd again broached the subject with Jonah. When Jonah had finally been convinced that this was truly what Sohel wanted, he'd agreed.

"Thank you, Sohel. I promise to make you proud."

Sohel had patted him on the shoulder. "You already do. Just don't forget Mrs. Wojtiski's triple bubble wrap."

Now Nath said, "I'm sorry, Mr. Walker." And he did sound genuinely regretful for Jonah's situation. "It happens more often than we would prefer that clients discuss something with their families and friends that they never put into place legally. And a signed and notarized will is truly an ironclad document."

"He showed me the will. He did take care of it legally."

"Unless he signed and notarized with two witnesses present—a process handled in our office," Nath said, not unsympathetically, "he didn't."

Jonah's mind raced with possibilities and his breath was still shallow in his tight chest. Had Sohel used a different attorney? Who would that be? Could there be two wills in existence? If so, wouldn't the one with the more recent date be honored?

Or—might Sohel have failed to complete the process?

Jonah rubbed his forehead with both hands and pushed his fingers into his temples as he cradled the phone between his ear and shoulder. The throbbing in his head continued.

"Additionally," Nath said, "you should know that although we are still working through paperwork, Mr. Gupta does not want responsibility of maintaining the building or dealing with a renter. He is listing the property."

———

The rest of the day passed in a haze of worry. A few more customers happened in. One was a local business owner who needed to reorder takeout menus. Another was an older man who always insisted on both faxing and mailing the same documents—in case one or another didn't arrive. Old school for sure. The third was a nearby resident who needed to overnight ship a passport to her son at college for an employment background check because he'd lost his license.

Jonah knew that Sohel would have taken great pleasure in each visit, so he made sure to put on a smile and help everyone just as he would have before the rotten blow he'd received today.

Still—the visits cemented the fact that he had to find a way to prove Sohel's intentions, so that Jonah could then honor his own promise to the man.

The one bright spot was that Willie Leon—*the* Willie Leon, lineman for the Pittsburgh Steelers, adored for his game-changing quarterback sacks—walked into the Print & Ship. He looked around and appeared a little confused when all he saw was racks of supplies, a wall of PO boxes, and a counter.

"Hey, man," Willie said, "you know anything about that art in the window?"

"I'm the artist. What do you want to know?" Jonah fought the urge to go all fan crazy on the poor guy.

"That one of Kennywood—is that the only size?"

"I can make one bigger, if you want."

"Yeah. For my son's birthday, for his room. Real big. He'd love that. Loves that damn park. Me? If I have to ride the Jack Rabbit one more time…" Willie groaned.

"I'm surprised you even fit in those old cars."

"I don't. That's the problem."

They had a good laugh over that, sorted out sizing, cost, and pickup, and then Willie left.

Holy shit. Willie Leon's kid would have one of Jonah's creations hanging over his bed!

Jonah walked on air for only a few minutes before reality hit.

None of Willie's teammates or friends or family would be buying any more of Jonah's art. None of his son's pals would be begging their parents for similar pieces. Nobody —famous or not—was going to be walking in off the street because they'd seen his art in the window and wanted to hang it over their bed or desk or even their guestroom toilet.

That was a huge problem. Jonah was only just becoming known for his art—in large part because of Sohel's willingness to showcase that art in one of the front windows.

The Print & Ship was in a key location in Pittsburgh's Strip District—arguably the neighborhood with the most foot traffic and the most tourists. And Jonah's graphic designs of famous and not-so-famous Pittsburgh landmarks and iconic idiosyncrasies appealed to both the natives and tourists alike.

But it wasn't just about Sohel's windows. It was Jonah's newfound pride.

While Jonah had always loved to draw and create, he hadn't been at this very long. He'd always loved to draw and wanted to go to art school—but putting together a portfolio had seemed daunting. He didn't fool himself into thinking he was all that talented anyway. His successful brothers, Jake and Jeremy, had both gotten practical degrees and made it look easy. Jonah had tried that route. But spending his parents' money and racking up his own debt didn't sit well when he couldn't figure out what the hell he'd wanted to do with his life.

He'd intended to go back to school, but one year had led into another, and next thing he knew, he'd been working for Sohel for ages. A couple of years ago, after Sohel's arthritis had gotten so bad that he could barely work a mouse, Jonah had taken over designing the business cards and flyers. He caught the bug and learned enough Adobe Illustrator to manage simple logos. Then he'd dived down the rabbit hole of Photoshop. He took a couple courses at a local college and simultaneously plowed through YouTube tutorials like he drank water after a workout. He played with effect after effect on landscapes, figures, scenery, icons, and anything that caught his interest—both during downtime at the shop and after hours.

The artist's soul that he'd managed to ignore erupted like a vomiting rainbow, and he started creating wild, colorful things just for fun. Eventually he'd narrowed to a signature style that was all his own.

Jonah went out to the sidewalk, stepping almost into the street to eyeball the front window. He often did this in order to decide which pieces he might swap out for newer ones, which would look right in place of something that had just sold, or what he was missing.

Sidewalks in the Strip were narrow and crowded. Jonah looked right through the people crossing in front of him.

Normally it was a rush to see so many of his pieces up there all together in the shop window, and his brain would fire with ideas. Today, that feeling eluded him. Dread and worry were taking up too much space.

Because it wasn't just the art and it wasn't just his pride—it was that he'd started earning real money. Not an hourly wage, but an actual living. He had only just begun discovering his own worth.

He wasn't going to tuck tail and slink off quietly. And he wasn't willing to give up his best shot at a true livelihood without a fight.

"Fuck that," Jonah said with all the vehemence he felt.

A woman crossing in front of him jumped, then glared.

"Sorry!" Jonah raised his hands.

Jonah navigated the pedestrian traffic and pushed back through the door.

He *had* to find the will that Sohel had shown him. Preferably before Kalpani and her jagoff cousin showed up again.

# 3

Kalpani dragged her depressed friend Darcy out to dinner, hoping to get her mind off her troubles. It was mid-December and the city was doing up the seasonal displays, events, and holiday music everywhere one turned —except for Darcy it only added insult to injury, because her relationship with Jeremy seemed to be over. Kalpani wasn't sure there was much hope, and she hurt for her friend. Darcy perked up when they discussed her role in Kalpani's future salon—but Kalpani knew even that was loaded. After her run-in with Jonah, she and Darcy had quickly put two and two together: Jonah and Darcy's Jeremy were brothers.

Kalpani already knew what she had to do, but she needed a moment and excused herself. She went to the ladies' room, washed her hands, and, as she was drying them, looked herself in the mirror. She puffed out her cheeks and blew out a harsh breath. Then she returned to the table, where Darcy pretended she hadn't been checking her phone to see if Jeremy had called.

Kalpani slid into her chair and pulled out her hand lotion. As she slathered it on, she said, "I want to offer you an out of the investment in Xanadu."

Darcy's eyebrows shot up.

"I know you're worried," Kalpani said. "If Jeremy does call you, finding out you are helping me oust his brother is only going to tank things again."

"You'd give up your dream on the slimmest chance Jeremy's going to call me?"

"Well, no. That building is everything as far as my dream goes. But I will absolutely let you off the hook and scramble to find an investor or two. The terms surely wouldn't be as good, but..." She shrugged. "I have some wealthy clients I could talk to." She'd been at a high-end salon downtown for years, and many of her clients had become friends.

Darcy smiled but shook her head. "I'm okay. If Jonah had that will, or any leg to stand on, any shot at all to get the building, I'd back out. But all signs point to that building being sold fast, and from what I know, it won't be Jonah bidding against you. Besides, I guarantee the damage is already done. If Jonah has even once mentioned your name—Jeremy knows Hellston Enterprises is helping you."

"Because he knows how close you and I are."

Darcy nodded. "And how strongly I feel about my work."

Other than Jeremy, her investment business was the most important thing to Darcy. Without him? It became that much more important to her friend. Kalpani let out a big breath she didn't even know she was holding. "Thank you."

They'd already paid the check, so they slipped into their winter coats and grabbed their purses. They exited the restaurant into the dark and cold and headed toward Kalpani's apartment. Darcy was parked just a block further away.

Kalpani felt Darcy looking at her and finally asked. "What?"

"You've never said why this salon is so important to you."

Just then, as they approached the front of Kalpani's building, Kalpani realized that even hidden under a large scarf covering her head and torso, she recognized the woman who'd just exited the glass door.

Kalpani called, "Meenu!"

The woman stopped, and the hunch of tension in her shoulders seemed to lift for a second—until she spotted Darcy.

"Hi," Kalpani said, and hugged her friend. She introduced Darcy and Meenu. "Where are the kids?"

"At home. They're fine." Meenu spoke too quickly. "It was good to see you." She turned to go, and Kalpani tugged on her sleeve. She wasn't wearing a coat, or socks, or makeup. Just that big silk wrap over a sweater, jeans, and sneakers—no match for the raw chill in the evening air.

"I've missed you." Kalpani did not want Meenu running off. Something was wrong—she could always tell. "Come into the lobby and get warm for a minute at least. You too," Kalpani told Darcy.

She didn't give Meenu a choice, simply buzzed them all in and tugged her inside. "How are the kids? Are they looking forward to Christmas? Your parents?"

Meenu supplied only single-word answers. Kalpani would have needed a magical spinning wheel to turn this into a real conversation. The harsh fluorescent light of the lobby made Meenu's normally warm-toned skin looked wan and dull. The dark circles under her shuttered eyes stood out too, and Kalpani's heart clenched.

*Durga,* she thought, *give Meenu strength.* It killed Kalpani that there was so little she could do to help her best friend. Maybe the Indian goddess known for strength had some ideas.

"I've got to go," Meenu said. "We, umm, ran out of formula." She rubbed her arms. "Idiot me forgot my wallet, so I'm going to have to go home and still try to make the pharmacy before it closes." She gave Kalpani a tight smile and told Darcy it'd been nice to meet her.

"Wait—" Kalpani dug in her purse. "You'll never make it home and back in time." Meenu wouldn't have been any more honest had Darcy not been here, but she wouldn't have run as fast. Kalpani pulled a hundred dollars from her wallet and pressed it in Meenu's hand.

"Thank you, I'll—"

"No rush," Kalpani cut her off. She didn't care about the money. Meenu hadn't yet paid her back, and she wouldn't likely be in a position to do so anytime soon.

Meenu ducked her head and skittered away, and Kalpani's shoulders dropped about three inches.

"Formula must be even steeper than I thought," Darcy said.

Kalpani shook her head, watching the door close but seeing the empty space Meenu used to fill.

Finally, she turned to Darcy. "You wanted to know

why?" Kalpani knew her voice was too fierce. "That's why. Women from my culture…"

She shook her head. Meenu's story wasn't hers to tell.

"Not every marriage is a bad one, though, surely."

"Of course not," Kalpani snapped. She offered Darcy an apologetic look and let out a breath heavy with frustration and sadness. "But it's rare for a woman to be independent or self-sufficient or even single—even here in the States. We're always secondary and invariably under a man's thumb. Father, then husband, and if the marriage is a bad one…" She shuddered. "It's still very…acceptable."

"That's…"

"Yeah." Kalpani thought again of her once-vibrant friend. Meenu had been college-educated, graduated summa cum laude with two degrees, accounting and economics, from Brown University. She'd even married outside of their culture—having pushed her parents to allow a love match.

"Can't see you under anyone's thumb," Darcy said. Then she grinned. "Pretty sure you'd take your favorite hair shears and aim for the heart."

Kalpani smiled. "And that is why I need to be a successful salon owner—so I don't end up in jail for murder."

"We'll make it happen," Darcy said.

"Damn straight." Kalpani was more thankful than ever for Darcy's support.

When Kalpani owned her own business, she'd be in a position to change things. She'd need an accountant, after all.

Saturday evening, Jonah tore the Print & Ship apart. No will.

On Sunday, he let himself into Sohel's apartment to look there. Sohel had given Jonah a key during his last hospital stay. He'd wanted his *chappals*—leather slippers —his own razor, and his book. Afterward, he'd suggested Jonah keep the key.

"If I don't show up at the shop in the morning," Sohel had said, "you can find me before the flies." He'd thought this funny, but Jonah hadn't appreciated the visual.

It appeared that Sohel's brother Ranji, or maybe his wife, had cleaned out the apartment of anything that would spoil—otherwise, the place looked much like it always did. Ranji had called Jonah to make sure he'd seen the announcement about Sohel's services. They were nice people. Jonah would be sure to offer the Guptas his help if they needed assistance moving furniture. He could easily enlist his brothers or some friends to help.

It was hard for Jonah to be in Sohel's private space, and he made quick work of looking through Sohel's desk, bedside table, and bookshelf for any stacks of papers or folders that looked like they could hold a will. No dice. Only a pained heart. He missed the old man terribly.

During the day Monday, he rifled through Sohel's old-fashioned Rolodex and called the number on every card that listed a law office. Some had used their printing services at one time or another, but none had recently handled a will for Sohel.

By Tuesday Jonah was out of ideas and tried to concentrate on simply running the shop and creating art.

He closed the Print & Ship early Thursday, in order to

shower and dress for the Thursday evening visitation hosted by the Gupta family at the funeral home.

Jonah picked up his mom en route. Rita Walker had fed Sohel almost as often as she'd fed Jonah over the years. Either they'd walk down to The Wanderlust for dinner after closing up, or she'd drop by with pints of soup just for Sohel.

She wrapped Jonah in a tight hug, her familiar mom smell making his eyes prickle.

"How are you holding up?" she asked, narrowing her eyes and scanning his face.

"It's been…" He shrugged. "Strange."

"As we both know, grieving goes through a lot of phases."

"Grief I can handle." He opened the car door for her, and she raised an eyebrow as she slid in.

Why had he said that? As Jonah rounded the car, he resigned himself to telling her everything. Well, not *every-thing*. The fact that he had the hots for Kalpani didn't matter at all.

Sure enough, when he started the car, she said. "Tell me." So, as he drove, he gave her the basics.

"Oh, hon." Rita patted his leg. "I'm so sorry. Did you look through Sohel's apartment, too?"

"Yes. Everywhere I can think of, I've looked."

Jonah parked in the lot of the Hillendorf Funeral Home. He turned the car off. "Are you gonna be okay?"

He hadn't been here since they'd buried his dad last spring. Hap Hillendorf, a longtime family friend had been as professional and supportive as possible, but the truth was that this place would now always hold memories of saying goodbye to Jonah's father. At least the actual funeral and subsequent luncheon tomorrow would be held at locations he was less familiar with.

Rita placed her hand in his and squeezed. Then she looked at the brick building and drew a long, shaky breath. "I'll have to be. You?"

He nodded.

They climbed out of the car, then took the stairs to the entrance. He held the door for his mom and sucked in a last breath of fresh air. He'd come to hate the smell of a funeral home.

They each signed the guest book then quickly became separated greeting Sohel's various friends and family. Jonah braced himself and stepped up to pay his respects to Sohel's brother and his wife. Ranji Gupta looked so much like Sohel, only a little younger and paunchier. His wife grasped Jonah's hand.

"Thank you for always being there for Sohel. He was lucky to have such a friend."

Jonah choked up, managing only a nod. He swallowed hard to keep his tears at bay and hastily pulled his hand from hers.

He spun—and found himself face to face with Kalpani.

Kalpani's lips parted in surprise, then her brown eyes went soft with empathy.

Fuck that. He didn't care who saw his raw emotion, but of all people, he sure didn't want *her* sympathy.

"Jonah," she said just above a whisper.

She looked extra classy this evening, wearing a black dress with a fitted top and flared skirt, tasteful makeup, and her hair smoothed to perfection. He felt a stir inside him. She was so damn pretty—

He clenched his jaw and shouldered past her.

He spotted Mrs. Wojtiski and made a beeline toward her. He could ask if her daughter had enjoyed the cookies.

Later, when the place had begun to clear out, Jonah joined his mom, who was looking at photos of Sohel and an album with various clippings.

Ranji put his hand on his shoulder. "Thank you both for coming tonight."

"Of course," Rita said. Then she excused herself so that Jonah and Ranji could talk.

Jonah offered to help Ranji with Sohel's apartment, specifically mentioning the heavy lifting. Ranji thanked him, then said, "You already know that I am going to sell the building."

Jonah nodded. He was sure that Ranji had been informed of the situation—or lack thereof—with Jonah and the Print & Ship via one grapevine or another. There wasn't much he could say about it without the paperwork in hand to prove his claim.

"I wanted to ask if you want any—or all—of the equipment from the shop—the computers and printers and such," Ranji said. "I would not know if I was getting a good price if I tried to sell them, and I think that Sohel would want you to take your pick."

"I—" Jonah shook his head. He had the odd sense that he was speaking with Sohel himself. Not only did the brothers look alike with their black-framed glasses and gray wisps of a combover, they also sounded alike, turning Ws into Vs.

The offer was generous, but he couldn't accept. At least not yet. Because where the hell would he store—let alone make use of—any of it without a space of his own?

"Thank you," Jonah said. "Let me think about it."

When the building sold, he'd lose not only the shop, but his living space above. It was one thing to bunk at his mom's for a while, but he would never go so far as to set up shop in her home—or anyone's. The enormous wide-format printer alone was a deal breaker. Not to mention his constant presence if he was living *and* working somewhere.

He had some savings. Sohel hadn't paid much when Jonah had started working there, but for a long while now, he'd been living rent-free above Sohel's business. That was another instance of Sohel cloaking a gift with his own practical needs. "You save me the cost of a security system. You being here means these old bones do not have to work so late."

The only big-ticket item Jonah had purchased recently was Sohel's car. Sohel rarely drove anyway, but when he failed his most recent eye exam, he'd insisted that Jonah take the vehicle for a few thousand less than it was worth. "You save me the trouble of dealing with the yahoos," he'd said.

But Jonah's savings weren't up to a down payment on a building. He doubted they'd even cover a year of rental space in such a hot spot. He felt the tension building in his forehead again and rubbed his fingers over one temple.

What in the hell was he going to do?

**4**

———

Kalpani felt lucky to have a good recommendation for a contractor—who also happened to be available to meet her in the Strip District and take a look at her building.

Yes, she was thinking of it as *her* building. She believed in the power of visualization. So she was picturing the perfect shade of gray on the walls, purple love seats with red accent pillows in the reception area, bold art on the walls pulling it all together, and hip metal tire-tread kick plates in front of each station. She tried to envision the sign spelling *Xanadu* over the front door—but she couldn't quite. It'd be something special, though.

Forget Olivia Newton-John and her roller skates and eighties styles. References in literature always painted Xanadu as a sumptuous and idyllic paradise or utopia. A place where dreams come true.

Kalpani's Xanadu would be exactly that. A place where clients could slink in with a rat's nest and shredded nails, pamper themselves silly, and walk out radiating confidence like Aishwarya Rai Bachchan or Beyoncé or Scarlett Johansson.

It was also, of course, where her own dreams were going to come true.

She stood tucked against a building's front, out of the way of the worst of the winter wind and the pedestrians streaming by. It was Saturday morning—the busiest time in the Strip—but she was working today and needed to squeeze this in between yoga and breakfast with her friend Darcy and her shift at the salon.

Kalpani sipped her coffee—glad she had it to warm her hands—and tried not to let her impatience show. The contractor, Lou, was already five minutes late.

She'd asked him to meet her on the corner in front of Mon Aimee Chocolate, rather than in front of the Print & Ship, because she didn't want to intrude on Jonah or cause any more discomfort than necessary. He'd looked so upset at Sohel's visitation service. The depth of his grief had her pressing her hand to her chest to stop the hurt.

On Friday morning at the funeral, they hadn't spoken, but she'd been very aware of how rigidly he held himself and knew he was holding his emotions carefully in check. For his sake, she would tread as lightly as she could.

Not that she could stop pushing to get a contract on the building as fast as possible, but still…the pain in Jonah's eyes. She'd had the strongest urge to lay her palm on his face, press her lips to his, and then tuck her head up under his chin and just hold on tight to him, offering what comfort and strength she could.

Lou appeared at her elbow, making her jump. He introduced himself, and she thanked him for coming.

"Sure thing," he said with an easy smile in a kind face.

He appeared to be about ten years older than her and was fit, with big, scarred hands, and had a backpack slung over one shoulder. He wore only a thick shirt, no jacket, and didn't seem the least bit bothered by the wind whipping from the river right down 21st Street.

"It's this way," she said, and headed for the crosswalk.

She and Lou weaved around weekend shoppers and Saturday tourists, making it impossible to discuss details. She tossed her coffee in a bin, then peeled off her gloves and dug in her purse for her favorite heavy-duty hand lotion as they waited at the corner. She was careful to work it into her dry knuckles and cuticles. The act was both soothing and protective. She frowned as she realized she felt like she was preparing herself for battle.

When they arrived at the door, she could see Jonah inside talking with someone at the counter. She paused, turning to Lou. "We might not get the warmest reception," she said.

He shrugged. "No worries. I've seen it all."

Good for him, but she was a little worried. She took a deep breath and pushed through the door.

Jonah looked up with a smile. As soon as he saw her, however, his eyes narrowed and his mouth flattened to a harsh line. He turned back to his customer—a very big guy.

Kalpani spoke in a hushed voice. "Obviously the reception area would be here in the front. The whole middle will be the stylists' stations."

"How many stations do you need?" Lou asked.

One of the reason's she'd chosen Lou was that he had some experience with salons. In fact, he was reputable enough that he seemed to have experience in nearly every commercial area.

"If we can fit them, ten."

He jotted that on a clipboard. "Sinks in the back, plus a prep room, right?"

She nodded. "There's a second floor, and I'll need three rooms that are private up there for massage and nails and such. There has to be storage space up there with built-in shelving. A small office would be great if we can fit it without sacrificing anything else."

He pulled a wheel from his pack. She slid a glance at Jonah, who was still involved with his customer. Lou walked to one wall and extended the handle—a rolling measuring tape. Cool.

She was aware of Jonah's low rumble as he explained something to the client. He gestured with one hand despite being in the middle of wrapping a giant rectangular something in bubble wrap and then brown paper.

The man thanked him in a voice even deeper than Jonah's.

And now, without the paper crinkling, she could hear his response. "Welcome. Just hope it doesn't end up a dartboard."

The client laughed. "No way. That happens, it's moving to my room." The client laughed, and when he turned, she realized just who it was: Willie Leon. No wonder she could barely see past him. He was one of the better-known players for the Steelers—a linebacker, no less.

Lou turned then, too. A big grin split his face. Willie headed for the front of the shop, and Lou jumped into action. "Let me get the door for you."

Kalpani glanced toward Jonah. "Wow," she said. "Willie Leon, huh? Very cool."

He came around the corner and bore down on her. "What are you doing?"

"I brought my contractor."

Air shoved out of his nose as he shook his head, making her think of a dragon—an angry one, gathering steam.

"You can't just chill for a few days?" A flush suffused his cheeks. "Give a guy time to get his head around this shit?"

Her own nostrils flared. "The timeline isn't in my control."

"Like hell it isn't."

"It isn't," she said. "My cousin is listing this property —probably as we speak—and I have to be ready with my bid. To do that, I need to know what my renovation costs will be."

He glared.

She looked away and saw that Lou was having an animated discussion with the athlete. It had been an exciting game on Monday night.

She took a deep breath. "Listen, I know you're dealing with a lot right now, but you need to come to terms—"

"You have no idea what I need."

She raised her chin. "Maybe not, but I do know that you are wasting your time running this shop. You should shut the doors and start planning for—"

"You need to leave."

"When they're done"—she angled her head to the duo outside—"we're going upstairs."

"No." Jonah's eyes were hard, his expression stony.

"Be reasonable."

He tilted his head to one side, then the other. "Nope. Not feeling remotely reasonable."

Dang it. She always got prickly when someone pushed her. Her big mouth always just pushed even harder—and obviously that was making this worse. She tried to rein things back in. "It won't take long. I promise. We just need some measurements."

"Too bad."

It took everything she had not to growl. Kalpani's fists were now clenched so hard that she realized she'd likely punctured her palm with a fingernail. That would sting all day at work tomorrow. She'd gone from wanting to make this as easy as possible on Jonah to wanting to throttle him.

She pulled herself to her full height—five four with the booties. "You do not own this building."

He grasped her elbow firmly and marched her toward the front door. In her heeled footwear, she didn't have the balance to do anything but go along, which really made her mad.

"What are you going to do? Just keep freeloading indefinitely?"

His eyes widened then went stark, and his lip curled in what she could only call a snarl.

Crap—why had she said that? Letting her temper run her mouth never went well, and she lashed out when push came to shove.

Jonah yanked open the door and pushed her through.

"Excuse me, Willie." Jonah's voice sounded so pleasant that she twisted her head to look at him. "My friend, Kalpani, asked to be introduced." Willie gave her a broad smile. Before either of them could speak, however, Jonah added, "Sorry. I hear the shop phone."

He darted inside, leaving her no choice but to play fangirl.

Turned out Willie was a lovely, gracious man. A total sweetheart despite his imposing size.

When the conversation had run its course, she turned to reenter the shop.

She tugged on the door handle, but it only moved far enough to make the bell above tinkle. Peering through the glass, she realized Jonah had disappeared.

"Let me," Lou said.

But Kalpani knew better. She put her hands on her hips and swore.

Her and her big mouth had suggested Jonah shut his doors. He'd one-upped her and locked them out.

**5**

———

S ohel's Print & Ship had a tiny kitchenette but only a
microwave to heat things, and the small room he
slept in above the shop had a TV but wasn't much of a
hangout. So, normally, Jonah would go out in the evenings
to meet friends, join his family for dinner, hit a hotspot for
some music, or head downtown for an event.

Saturday night, however, Jonah chose to lie low. After
stewing all day over Kalpani's visit, he wasn't fit for
company. If he went to The Wanderlust for a delicious free
dinner, his mom would demand to know what he was
gnawing on—as his father used to say. Likewise getting
out and drinking himself into oblivion for free at his
brother Jeremy's club. It might be too loud to talk, but
he'd still be miserable. Because right this second,
accepting generosity from anyone felt shitty—even from
family.

After closing up for the day—for real, not just locking
out Kalpani and hiding from her like a coward—he hit the
street. He wore a ski cap and reflective shades. He buried

his hands deep in his pockets and kept his head down and his feet moving fast.

It wasn't December's raw chill. For once, he would prefer to appear as unapproachable as possible in this neighborhood, where a five-minute walk always took him ten because he knew nearly every business owner and resident.

He drove to Edgar's Best Tacos for takeout. That he could *buy*. With his *earned money*.

*Dammit.*

He wasn't a freeloader or a squatter—no matter what it looked like to someone who couldn't possibly know what kind of relationship he and Sohel had shared. But it ate at him anyway. Did all Sohel's friends and family think that?

He gritted his teeth and decided he'd also hit the liquor store for something stronger than the beer he kept in the shop's mini fridge.

Jonah wasn't that hungry when he returned to the shop, so he set the takeout bag on the counter. He eyed the Maker's Mark bourbon he'd bought but decided to crack open a beer instead to start. Then he pulled out the stool and woke up the iMac. He opened the piece he'd been working on before Willie Leon and then Kalpani and her contractor had shown up.

It was a shot he'd taken of the ice-skating rink and tree at PPG Place's Courtyard. He'd been trying to keep up with the various holiday events around town—the Christmas Village, Freeze Fest, the tree at Point State Park, and more—thinking that if he could work fast, he might just sell them fast. Christmas gifts, right?

If he also printed up some in a five-by-seven-inch size, he could wrap them on a deeper frame, and they'd stand free. He wouldn't even need to brace small stretcher frames like those. They'd take no time at all. They'd make nice hostess gifts or a good choice for those exchange things people did. What'd they call them? White elephants or secret Santas?

The skating rink piece needed to be run through a series of effects, and then he needed to make the colors pop. But first there were a few figures he wanted to remove. Photoshop made that fairly easy, but he always finalized the adjustments by hand. It took concentration but not brainpower, and he let his mind wander.

Back to Kalpani, of course. Why'd she always have to look so good? Shiny ebony hair that he longed to touch, high cheekbones, big eyes that begged for his camera, that lilting voice coming from those plump pink lips—both of which he wanted right next to his ear murmuring words of encouragement as he—

*Shit.*

He had to stop this. Those lips weren't ever going to whisper sexy things in his ear. Kalpani preferred barbs that cut deep.

That night they'd kissed and kissed? He'd liked her fun, sparkly personality—and he'd also thought she seemed like a good person. They'd talked for hours and really bonded. At the time he assumed he'd see her again, was sure they were at the very least headed for a first date, if not something lasting. But apparently his instincts had been wrong. She'd walked away like those hours had meant nothing.

Now, it was clear she didn't hold him in very high regard. That was a giant neon sign. Jonah had to push Kalpani out of his thoughts once and for all.

Jonah finished removing the last of the figures on the skating rink. He zoomed out again and looked at the whole. It worked, but…he wasn't feeling it. Normally, he could sink into a design and find that hours had passed, but tonight? Well, he didn't trust his gut.

Kalpani—damn her—had thrown him. And too much was eating at him—all the unresolved issues, so much murky and unknown facing him.

Jonah hit save, then stood and stretched. He opened his taco dinner and took a few bites.

Insanely good, but he was going to need some paper towels. He went to the kitchenette on the other side of the wall. He opened the cupboard where they kept paper products and found both an ink cartridge and a box of condiments.

"Sohel." He smiled thinking of Sohel's complete inability to stay organized.

*Wait—holy shit.*

Jonah moved back a few feet to stare at the wall of cupboards. He'd looked in all the places Sohel *should* have stashed paperwork.

What he needed to do was search all the other places.

There was hope yet.

Jonah yanked open another kitchen cabinet and then another, pulling things down and out, making sure he could see every dark corner before he gave up on a space. He found manuals for equipment that had crapped out fifteen years ago, a hairbrush and crusty tin of pomade, a stash of Indian pop music on cassette tapes, and so many more things that shouldn't be stored in a kitchen. At one point, he dug out a few large trash bags, knowing that if he could at least trash anything that was clearly not salvageable, his workload would be less later. Mainly, though, he just attacked every nook and cranny like a maniac, shaking his head or laughing now and then.

When he'd gotten through every single kitchen cabinet, he ran upstairs. Jonah's room was his own, and he knew there were no papers in the bathroom vanity. But there was an odd linen cabinet up there to check, not to mention the back room. He'd checked the obvious spots in there, but now that he was thinking straight—or thinking like Sohel, anyway—he wanted to look again.

Finally, Jonah braced his arms on the doorframe of the back room and hung his head. He'd worked up a sweat and was breathing hard. He'd been sure that tonight he'd hit pay dirt…and nada.

"Dammit."

Jonah trudged back downstairs, completely dejected. He checked the lock on the back door, headed for the kitchen—and stopped.

Slowly he turned around. At the back door. The coat closet—or, rather, the junk catcher.

Jonah lunged forward and pushed the sliding door to one side. It was a closet Jonah normally avoided—literally never opened because it was likely to erupt. Rubber rain-boots, old coats, a ratty comforter, a pile of Terrible Towels, numerous broken umbrellas, an enormous tangle of wire hangers, a huge stack of phonebooks from floor to about waist high, a bolt of floral cotton fabric—*for what exactly, Sohel?*

He slid the doors the other way. A stash of candy bars and one of canned vegetables. A genie hat—Sohel's idea of Halloween. And a three-foot Santa the old man had always dragged out during the holidays. No will jumped out at him, so Jonah started grabbing stuff from the top and worked his way down.

Hanging on a hook on the side wall, under a ball cap and a knit cap and a sweatshirt, was a plastic grocery bag that felt like it held—*hopefully*—papers.

Jonah held his breath and peered inside.

Dear God, he'd found it.

"Woohoo!" he yelled, and then leapt over the pile of junk he'd dumped in the middle of the walkway and ran to the front for more light.

He tore off the bag, removed the clip holding the sheaf together—thinner than he would have expected—and flipped quickly to the rear pages where he knew signatures would be.

His breath let out in a whoosh, his shoulders sank, and his knees nearly gave way.

"Oh, Sohel."

The signature lines were blank.

But Jonah had seen enough to realize that there was writing—Sohel's notes—all over it.

Jonah tapped the papers on the counter so the stack was tidy, then laid it down carefully. He unearthed a glass from the mess in the kitchen, added ice cubes from the mini fridge, and poured a healthy amount of Maker's Mark.

Then he took the drink and the will to the cushioned chair in the corner—the one Sohel often rested in—and began to read.

This was a preliminary version of the will, likely the very same copy Sohel had showed Jonah. A copy that had definitely never gotten as far as a second pass, let alone a notary's stamp. Sohel had certainly read it line for line, given the penciled questions in the margins, circled words, and underlined phrases. But he must have gotten distracted —likely put it in that bag to take home and set it near the back door, where it eventually got pushed aside. Maybe he thought if he hung it with his hat, he'd remember to take it with him—home or to the law firm.

Jonah sat for a long time, hearing Sohel's voice clear as day as he read the man's questions and followed his thoughts.

Little by little he let go of Sohel's wishes that he continue on here, put aside what could have been, and began to wrap his head around starting over.

Then he toasted Sohel, and finally let himself really cry over the loss of his friend.

---

Jonah woke hard Sunday morning having dreamed of gorgeous, infuriating Kalpani—again. And wasn't it some bitter icing on the cake that his body wanted someone who thought so little of him. He swore, punched his pillow, and then flipped onto his back to stare at the ceiling.

Other than being pissed at his body's refusal to see reason, however, he was in decent shape despite the crying and the bourbon. In fact, he felt more clearheaded than he had since Sohel had died.

All because he'd found the will last night.

It didn't matter what Kalpani or anyone else thought. Jonah knew where he'd stood with Sohel and was grateful for their relationship and the years they'd spent together. Jonah was honored that Sohel had wanted to entrust him with his business and customers, even if it wasn't to be.

Jonah's stomach growled, and he remembered that he had never returned to his takeout last night. He threw off his tangled covers and rolled to a sitting position.

Although things hadn't turned out the way Sohel had once wished—last night's discovery solidified the fact that there were some promises that weren't in Jonah's power to keep—Jonah could do what was right and act in Sohel's— now his brother's—best interests.

He thought of locking Kalpani and her contractor out and grimaced.

Time to man up. Starting now, he had to quit feeling sorry for himself. There was no alternate will that was going to save the day. The Print & Ship would be on the market soon—if it wasn't already. And it would sell fast. Jonah needed to give Ranji an answer about the equipment before he ended up tossed out on his ass with nothing.

It didn't matter if he felt like he had no direction. Today, he had to move forward. One step at a time. He needed to sort out a plan—even if it wasn't a great one.

Jonah showered, dressed, and walked over to The Wanderlust with his mind spinning. He kissed his mom and Sadie, who were both hustling to seat people, take orders, and deliver food. He greeted a few customers he knew well but headed to the kitchen as fast as he could without being rude.

"Hey, bro," Jake said from behind the grill. He set down a spatula and met Jonah halfway for a quick embrace. They'd talked a couple of times but hadn't seen each other recently. Jonah was sure Rita had filled in both his brothers after she'd gotten the whole scoop from him during the ride home from the funeral Friday.

Jake asked, "How are you holding up?"

Jonah angled his head toward the cooktop. "I'll be just fine if you can squeeze in another Black and Gold." That was a special omelet their Dad had concocted years ago, and Jonah loved the burnt bacon crumbles coupled with the Kerry Gold cheese.

"You got it," Jake said.

Jonah poured himself an orange juice and a cup of coffee. "You need help?"

"From you? No way." Jake winked.

Jonah could cook—it was like learning to walk in his family—but he lacked the focus that kept a busy morning at the diner running smooth. Of course, his brothers never missed a chance to remind him of it.

Jonah didn't care. He'd rather not help, especially today. "Cool by me. I'll be in the office."

The office was a small wood-paneled room off the kitchen where his mom and dad stored years' worth of payroll and vendor and tax info.

He set his OJ on the desk then took a slurp of his coffee as he looked around. There were pictures on the wall of his whole family in the diner. His dad wearing his favorite bandana pirate-style, singing his heart out in the kitchen. His mom posing with her sister Reenie in front of what he thought of as the travel wall (a wall full of postcards and pictures from customers who had slaked their own wanderlust). Jake with his arm around one of the longtime dishwashers. Jeremy hauling boxes up the cement dock stairs outside. Even Sadie, Jake's wife, laughing at the over-the-top flirting of old Mr. Salvatore when she was still in high school. And then Jonah, at maybe age four, squirting ketchup on a hot dog with the utmost concentration.

Jonah sucked in a deep breath. Nothing had changed in this room at all. He felt his dad's presence here, just as strongly as he felt Sohel's at the Print & Ship.

He drank another sip of coffee and then riffled through stacks of paper on the desk until he found a pad. He plucked a pen from a mug he'd made for his dad when he was about six.

He snorted. He'd liked bright colors even then—red ketchup on a white bun counted—but thankfully his skill had matured.

He wrote PLAN and underlined it. He stared at the page, nothing coming to mind. He began to doodle a series of flowing swirls but was saved when Jake hollered from the kitchen. Jonah jumped up to retrieve his omelet.

Rita was there, too, transferring plates from the warmer to her tray, and she nodded at the commercial toaster. "That rye just coming out is yours, too." Rita never forgot someone's favorites.

"Thanks." He smiled and gave her another kiss on the cheek. "You want me to carry that?"

She swatted him. "Certainly not. Eat while it's hot. If it gets much busier, though, we might have to press you into service. We're down a server today."

"No problem." Jonah buttered his toast, snagged his omelet from Jake, grabbed a fork and a napkin, and escaped into the office again.

His stomach rumbled happily as he forked bites into his mouth. Jake was just as good a chef as their dad had been.

Jonah eyed a picture of his dad. "Not that I'd tell you that."

He flipped the sheet and started over.

*Buy garbage bags.*
*Clean out shop.*
*Alert customers.*
The list went on from there in no particular order. Print & Ship tasks were straightforward. He didn't need to keep much other than materials and tools for printing, building stretcher frames, and then wrapping and shipping his art. He'd clear that with Ranji, but Jonah was ninety-nine percent sure the man wouldn't care.

The act of writing itself jump-started his brain, and he went back to the first page. But the word PLANS froze him up again. He started a clean sheet and titled it OPTIONS.

Less intimidating. Nothing was set in stone. Everything was just something to consider at this point. This list was all about how to keep selling art and bringing in income from it. He wrote:

*Talk to shopkeepers about renting window space*
*Create website*
*Determine which equipment is essential*
*Look into renting workspace/retail space*
*Apartment hunt*
He took a bite of toast and sat back in the chair. How fast could he find somewhere to live that wasn't a pit? Now that he was holding his head high, he wanted somewhere decent. He didn't want to take the first thing to come along, which meant he might have to talk to his mom about staying at her place for a while.

Everything in him resisted that idea. It would buy him time, yes—but if he couldn't work, he'd end up stuck there. Workspace was the priority, then, even if he had to live in a hovel or put a mattress under his framing table.

He went back to the list.

*Check savings account / consider loan*

*Business cards*

*Flyers*

Damn. The website would have to be done first—in order to show the web address on the printed pieces. He'd need access to the computers and printers. Which meant he'd better get that done before Kalpani or some other buyer swooped in.

Jonah started to feel overwhelmed, every piece of the puzzle depending on another. He rubbed his temples, decided more caffeine was in order, and carried his dishes to the kitchen.

"Hon, I need you," Rita said as she burst through the door.

He took the overloaded bus bin from her. "Where do you want me?"

Jonah spent the next two hours run far too ragged to think.

When he returned to the diner's office to rip off his lists from the pad and head back to the Print & Ship, he had a little more clarity.

It was Sunday. Not a good day to call on other business owners or reach out to customers, but an ideal time to sort out what equipment he really needed and clean up some of the mess he'd made last night. He could also draft a letter to thank customers for their many years of loyalty to Sohel and explain about closing up shop. And hopefully he could begin to create a website.

Side bonus? Sunday surely meant he was safe from one of Kalpani's unexpected visits.

**6**

————

On Sunday, Kalpani automatically called out a greeting as she walked through the door into the narrow entryway of her parents' apartment.

Her mother's head popped around the doorway of the kitchen. "Be quiet, *beta.*" A fond child's nickname, right along with a child's scolding. Chetana pointed her wooden spoon at the far corner of the living room.

Kalpani sucked in a quick breath and checked to see which patient was visiting her father. *Please not Meenu.*

Her shoulders sank with relief. She couldn't entirely see past her father—but the woman was older and wide. *Thank you, Waheguru.*

Ever since Kalpani could remember, her father had worked in a hospital and been responsible for all the ordering and restocking of supplies—everything from gauze to light bulbs. But he'd been a doctor before emigrating. His own community trusted him with their health. Plus, they were pleased not to pay exorbitant fees, offering what they could. No appointments; they simply showed up evenings and weekends. Her father always pushed patients toward a doctor or hospital if the issue was serious enough—but often there were matters people wanted to keep as private as possible.

Kalpani averted her eyes, shed her coat, knit cap, and gloves, and joined her mother in the kitchen.

"Hi, *Mummyji*," Kalpani said, though she was distracted by her father's patient.

"It is Auntie Urvi again only," Chetana said with the speech pattern elder Indians often used. Kalpani breathed even easier. Auntie—not related—wasn't so much a hypochondriac as a lonely older woman who used the visits as social hour.

Kalpani had dreaded patients coming since her seventh birthday. She remembered sitting on the floor, trying to plait colored string into her new doll's hair, when one of her father's regular patients stumbled in. The woman didn't see Kalpani tucked into the corner and therefore didn't hide her face as she often did. The area around her eye was swollen and already turning ghastly colors. But it was the globe of red nestled inside—looking for all the world like she'd shoved a red bouncy ball into her eye socket—that Kalpani had had nightmares about for years. Even at that young age, she understood that the woman had not fallen down the stairs *again*.

At the time, Kalpani and her dolls whispered an oath to each other never to allow an arranged marriage. But as she matured, she realized that arranged marriages were not the cause. Some even worked out well. The larger culture— especially when ethnically insulated or isolated—carried long-held beliefs of subservient women.

Meenu was a case in point. And Kalpani had been

worrying over her friend. She'd tried and tried to reach her since Wednesday. But Meenu never answered and hadn't returned her calls.

Kalpani sighed and reached for the pot on the stove that always held chicken *mukni,* or butter chicken. She lifted the lid, stuck her finger in, and then licked it.

Her mother swatted her—luckily not with a dirty spoon, which she wasn't above.

"You know I can't resist."

Chetana smiled. "Help me with the *bhartha.*"

No chore, that. Kalpani happened to love the spiced eggplant dish, and part of the reason she was here was to ease the burden on her mother, who did the bulk of the week's cooking on Sundays.

Kalpani washed her hands at the sink and got busy, the familiar tasks and distinctly Indian smells helping to continue the train of thought her father's patient had launched.

She chopped with more force than necessary. Sometimes she wished her parents would just order out, or maybe make grilled cheese or something once a week. Their marriage was a good one, but despite her mother's education and job, she played second fiddle to Kalpani's father. He wanted only his wife's home-cooked meals, but they also needed the income she brought in.

For Kalpani, too, her mother's job had been important. Kalpani would often sit in the car and wait with the cleaning crew as businesses closed up shop for the evening. Often, she saw American women coming out of a salon—smiling, confident, shiny—like they could take on the world. Then the stylists would exit looking capable in their sleek black clothing, counting their cash. To her, it looked like a lot of money.

In the Indian culture, parents pretty much pushed their children to three careers only: doctor, engineer, or lawyer. That meant a topnotch education first—preferably an Ivy League one. But Kalpani wasn't blind. Even those degrees and careers weren't infallible. Companies downsized. People were passed over for promotions. And, oh yes, prejudice still thrived.

The salons and other places that her mother cleaned gave Kalpani a glimpse of alternatives: trades and cash businesses where a person might have more control over their own success. A first-generation Indian girl like her didn't *have* to be dependent on a father or a husband or even a boss.

The idea, at first, was shocking. But the need for complete independence grew inside Kalpani as if it had weaved itself into her very bones.

Chetana turned a sizzling burner off, then the noisy hood fan.

"There, *beti*, now you can tell me about your week," her mother said.

"Not much to tell, just working," Kalpani said. She hadn't yet mentioned the opportunity of Sohel's shop to her parents. They would be horrified at the use of her savings and believe the risk was too great.

Heck—she was concerned herself. She feared the listing price—which still hadn't been decided, as far as she knew—could skyrocket in a bidding war. The numbers Ajay had been spouting—rubbing his hands together in glee as he mentally tallied his own commission—were terrifying. Even with Darcy's help, there was only so far Kalpani could stretch.

Just then from the living room, Auntie's chatter caught her ear. "Suraj says that Rama said that Ranji Gupta is not pleased with the real estate people. He does not like to deal with them, but he feels he has little choice if he does not want to be saddled with Sohel's building."

Kalpani's heart rate kicked up a notch.

She had thought that Ranji was committed to the idea of listing the building. But if not…she could simplify the process for him and save him some money in fees and commissions. And it'd certainly eliminate her worry about being edged out.

"*Mummyji,* excuse me for a minute."

Kalpani rushed to the bedroom she had shared with her siblings and dialed Darcy.

"Hey," Darcy said. "What's up?"

In a rush, Kalpani told her the idea.

"It's a great idea. Go for it!" Darcy sounded almost as excited as Kalpani felt.

"But I still don't know what the renovation cost will be, since Jonah wouldn't let my contractor take all the measurements or go upstairs."

"I'm sure we can figure something out, even if the number is higher than you hope," Darcy said.

Kalpani clenched the phone. Big amounts of money didn't worry her wealthy friend Darcy, but they scared Kalpani big time. She paced the tight room. "I'll give it one more shot with Jonah first."

"How? What are you going to say?"

"I have no idea." But Kalpani knew that, first and foremost, she needed to apologize. She'd said an awful thing to Jonah. It didn't matter if he was freeloading or not, and it was none of her business, but it was rotten of her to say it to his face.

"Let me know," Darcy said. "If you don't get anywhere, we'll just give it our best guess."

"Okay. Darcy? Thanks for being in my corner," Kalpani said.

Now, if only she could get Jonah in her corner, too.

———

Jonah was knee-deep in boxes and trash bags in the back of the Print & Ship when he heard the bell jingling repeatedly over the shop door. He'd had music playing and reached for his phone. Had someone been trying to reach him? He'd just seen his mom and Jake at The Wanderlust this morning. Nope, no calls.

Strange. It was late Sunday afternoon, and he was sure he hadn't scheduled basketball with Jeremy or anything with friends.

He stood, then groaned as his back protested. He'd been bending over for hours. He slugged some water and headed from the kitchen to the front of the shop.

*Kalpani.* A thrill shot through him and his achy back was forgotten, despite the fact that the situation meant he should probably dread seeing her.

What was it about this woman?

Through the glass he could see that she was carrying a foil-wrapped packet and was dressed down. Jeans and sneakers showed below a parka and a knit hat.

He wore an old t-shirt and torn jeans and was probably

covered in dust and grime, but whatever. She for damn sure wasn't here to ask him to prom.

Just yesterday he would have pretended he hadn't seen her, hadn't heard the door, or wasn't home. But in finding the will, he'd somehow reached a turning point. He found himself releasing the lock and pushing open the door.

Still, he was wary. Rather than inviting her in, he stood in the doorway. Instead of greeting her, he raised his eyebrows.

"Hi," she said, and he realized she was also wearing less makeup than usual. It made her look younger and sweeter. Less aggressive for sure—though that could have been her contrite expression. "Samosas. Homemade." She shoved the foil-wrapped package at him. "I didn't make them, my mother did. They're amazing. She's a great cook."

His omelet at The Wanderlust was a long time ago, and now he realized he'd forgotten to eat since. His suddenly rumbling stomach made him reach automatically to accept the offering, and he found it was both warm and smelled great.

"Can I come in?" He didn't answer right away, and she added, "I want to apologize."

She looked earnest, and he stepped back, holding the door for her. She moved a few steps into the room and twisted her hands together. No, not twisting, he thought. Working them as if she worked lotion into her skin.

He set the food on the shop counter—wow, it really did smell amazing—then turned back to face her.

"I'm really sorry about what I said—what I implied—yesterday." She'd been looking him in the eye, but now her gaze dropped. "I was out of line."

Jonah wasn't sure what to say. The freeloader comment had definitely burned, but whatever, he was a big boy and he was over it. "Okay. Thanks."

"When I get mad, I say stupid things I wish I could take back. I'm also sorry for being so pushy." She trailed off, then wrapped her arms around herself. "It's just that…" She looked at her feet, then up again. "I have a plan. And goals. It's my dream, really—to own my own salon."

Kalpani looked nervous, but her eyes shone, Jonah realized. Man, she was pretty. She changed directions as swiftly as wind that heralded a coming storm: unpredictable and sometimes fierce. But he remembered she'd intimated at this goal when they'd sat under that big oak talking for hours.

"And this building is my best shot. My *only* shot for a long while, probably." She took a big breath and then spread her arms out. "I'm hoping to make Ranji an offer— now, before it's listed. Otherwise, it will likely end up out of my reach."

He got it. This building, old and run-down as it was, sat on a prime piece of the Strip District. The location alone would cost a pretty penny. But the place would have to be renovated, and that would cost dearly, too. He turned and walked back over to Kalpani.

"I knew Sohel, too," she said. "Not as well as you probably did. But I think he would have preferred that his shop end up with someone like me, rather than some moneybags owner or some chain."

Jonah drew a deep breath. She wasn't wrong. And honestly—if he took his own needs out of the equation? Jonah would prefer that, too.

She linked her hands together. "I'm asking, please, if I might get those measurements so I can figure out what a fair and reasonable—but hopefully affordable—price would be. I can only borrow so much from my friend, Dar—"

She broke off, her eyes darting away.

*Ho, whoa…* "Darcy? Hellston?"

This was rich. Darcy was the love of his brother's life. She'd also invested in his club, Vine, and smashed his heart to smithereens—again—when she broke his trust. What a small, sucky world…

"Yes." Kalpani winced. "She's one of my best friends. I asked her if she'd be willing to help me, and she's agreed to invest in my salon. This was before we put two and two together."

He spun and moved a few steps away. Damn, there was always another crap on his cracker lately. He rubbed his temple with one hand and put the other on his hip. Did it even matter? No.

He nearly jumped when Kalpani's hand landed on the bare skin of his forearm.

"I'm sorry," she said, squeezing slightly.

He couldn't move, just stared at her hand. He'd imagined her touch so many times—but not like this, not in timid apology. He had such an urge to cover hers with his own, then lift it to his lips.

She dropped her hand and retreated.

He sucked in a breath, then blew it out.

*Okay.* So, it seemed this situation was going to be roses for everybody but him. This wasn't a movie. There was no change of fortune coming. He wasn't even going to get the girl in the end.

But it wasn't Kalpani's fault, or Darcy's, or Ranji's, or anyone's. It just was what it was. Still…

Jonah turned to face her and saw she was slightly pink in the cheeks.

She looked at his arm, before her eyes slid over his chest and away. She seemed to be avoiding his eyes and trying to avoid his body, too.

"So," he said, "you want me to let your contractor in to check out the whole place—probably down to the plumbing and electric box."

Her gaze flew to his and her face came alive. What he wouldn't give to be responsible for that look. She nodded.

"And you'd like that to happen as fast as possible."

She nodded again, and her hands came together almost in a prayer position.

"What's in it for me?"

Her eyes widened and she bit her lip. "As in…" Her gaze dropped to his jeans.

"Oh shit," he said, "no, I didn't mean— Not that I wouldn't want—" *Double shit.*

He rolled his eyes to the ceiling, filled his chest with air, and tried to fill his brain with oxygen. He looked at her again. "Let's be clear: I did not mean to imply anything sexual."

Her cheeks grew pinker, and damn if all he could think of now was having her under him, over him, everywhere, fulfilling every hot fantasy he'd ever had featuring her.

"I meant…" What did he mean? He hadn't even thought this through. "How about a glass of water?"

"Okay," she said. "Please."

He snatched up one of the high stools and moved it to the customer side of the counter. He gestured for her to sit, then slipped into the back room, weaving around bags of discards and boxes of goods to donate and filled two glasses with water at the sink.

He returned, set both down, and pulled out another stool from behind the counter. He placed it at a right angle to her, rather than facing her directly. It seemed less formal somehow.

"Thanks," she said, and took a sip.

He rested his arms on the counter. "The thing is, I had plans, too. And now, with Sohel gone, they are all shot to hell."

She was watching him carefully, almost warily. It occurred to him that maybe she thought this was going to be a monetary request—like taking a cut or something.

"I don't know if you realize, but I live upstairs."

Her mouth opened in surprise, and she looked upward as if she could see through the ceiling.

"With the sale of this building, I'm out of both a place to live *and* a place to work."

She stilled. "Oh."

"Yeah, *oh.*" He rolled his shoulders. "Ranji Gupta has offered me the equipment, but"—he gestured to the wide-format printer, the giant standing copier, and the whole series of computer and printers that sat on counters along the walls—"as you can see, I can't just crash anywhere. I need time to find the right space."

Her eyebrows drew together.

"I was thinking, if you are the buyer, that maybe you'd let me store this stuff upstairs for a while."

She opened her mouth.

"Just until I find some sort of studio."

"I'd planned to renovate the whole place at once,

but…" She nodded. "Maybe if you could pile it all at one end up there? So I only have a section left to do?"

"I'd be cool with that. And who knows, maybe I'll find something before you even start renovating."

"Okay then, if I'm the buyer—" She stopped and shook her head, a grin playing about the corners of her mouth. "As soon as I own this building, storage space upstairs is yours if you need it."

She stuck out her hand, and he grasped her warm palm in his. They shook once firmly, but neither let go. A smile bloomed on her face, lighting her eyes.

Jonah smiled back, but he suddenly had the sense that this bargain—while helpful for his future—might be really troublesome for his heart.

**7**

———

Four days later, Kalpani returned to the Strip District and headed for Jonah's shop. She shook her head at herself. She didn't know when she'd started thinking of it as Jonah's instead of Sohel's. And she didn't know when she'd start truly thinking of it as hers.

But it was time to do just that.

"It's mine, really mine," she said in wonder with a smile splitting her face. The passersby on Penn Ave didn't notice that she was talking to herself, but she wouldn't have cared anyway. The shop was *hers*.

She'd given Ranji a call as soon as it was decent on Monday morning—fearing that he'd sign on with the real estate agency before she could get her affairs in order. He'd graciously agreed to hear her out before he did anything. On Monday afternoon, as promised, Jonah had let her contractor poke his nose into every nook and cranny of the building. Lou had worked fast to give her a number, and then she and Darcy had worked just as fast to come up with a bid that Ranji Gupta wouldn't be able to refuse—

and yet one that Kalpani could live with. On Wednesday, she'd visited the Guptas, proposal in hand.

Today, Ranji had phoned her. "I have slept on it, and I happily accept. Sohel would be pleased."

She'd gushed her thanks, hung up the phone, and then shouted with joy. Thank goodness she'd happened to still be at home when he called, and not at the salon, because moments later, she'd collapsed onto her bed and sobbed.

She'd wanted this so badly. Of course, to some degree the reality was a little scary—using up her savings, incurring debt, owning a business, being responsible for not just her own livelihood but for others… Her parents were horrified when she'd told them what she was doing— which she had done before visiting the Guptas. Otherwise they'd hear it through the neighborhood grapevine before she even had an answer.

But fear wasn't what had her so emotional. There was no way she would allow herself to fail. She would do whatever it took to ensure success. This was her ticket right on past the scenario so many women, especially women of her culture, found themselves in. And in helping herself, she hoped she'd be able to help others as well.

Her tears were pure, overwhelming relief. Now, she would never, ever need to be reliant on a man. Her future was one hundred percent her own.

Just before she was about to cross the street to the Print & Ship—her salon!—her phone vibrated for the third time. She sighed. It was Ajay. She was going to have to deal with him sooner or later, and she didn't want it ringing constantly when she was talking to Jonah.

She stopped walking, peeled off one glove to answer

the call, and pressed herself up against a wall of a building, directly across from the shop.

Forgoing a greeting, Ajay said, "What the hell, Kalpani?"

She gritted her teeth. "You know you would have done the same."

"I took you down to the shop. I told you about it."

"And you would have gleefully taken the highest bidder and passed me over in the end. Besides, this isn't all on me. Ranji wasn't happy with your agency."

"He would have been happy when he got the best price."

"That's where you are wrong. It's not always about the money."

Kalpani hung up and tried not to let Ajay get to her. She'd spoken the truth. Ranji didn't care for the agency, didn't want to deal with them, and he was pleased to sell directly to someone like her—someone from his and Sohel's own community who might not get this chance otherwise. She hadn't signed anything with Ajay, and he—of all people—would truly have done the same in her position.

She shoved her phone back in her pocket and tried to shake off the exchange. If possible, at some point she'd send her dear cousin a client in order to make it up to him.

Jonah had spotted her and waved from inside the shop, and she brightened. She weaved through pedestrians and crossed the street.

When she entered the Print & Ship, he said, "So?"
"It's mine!"
He threw his arms up and then bounded toward her.

She expected a hug, but he scooped her up and spun her around. They were both laughing when he set her down.

She brushed her hair out of her face even as she thought that the only thing better would have been a celebratory kiss from him. "You're crazy."

"Nah, I'm just happy for you," he said, grinning, "and I don't have any champagne."

She laughed again.

How wonderful to be with someone happy for her— even though he was probably the last person that should be. He should be pissed off or bitter or at least bummed out, because the faster the transaction moved, the quicker he'd find himself out of this space.

Almost as if he read her mind, he said, "So what's the timeline?"

"The banks have to do their thing, but Lou says he can squeeze me in for January. He'd like to complete the project before his business heats up in the spring, so he sounds motivated."

Jonah nodded. "Probably after New Year's, then."

"Yes, I'd say so. I did talk to the contractor about our arrangement," Kalpani said. "Lou doesn't want the liability of any people here while it's torn up and potentially dangerous, but he doesn't care about stuff in storage. He'll keep the door shut or seal off the space to keep the dust out."

"Cool, thanks."

She looked around. "So, you have a couple of weeks to get all this upstairs."

"It's doable. Even with the holidays in there." He winked. "At least Santa will still know where to find me."

"And what are you asking for this year?"

"Besides a place to live and a place to work?"

Kalpani winced, but Jonah didn't look upset. In fact, he'd seemed to have reclaimed the easygoing nature that had attracted her to him in the first place. She decided to play along. "Anything elves could handle? New socks?"

"Afraid not. My most secret wish is very complicated." His gaze fell to her lips, and then he held her eyes. His twinkled, and Kalpani felt her face heat. Jonah was flirting with her.

They'd been at war to some degree since she'd first walked into his shop a couple of weeks ago. He hadn't flirted with her since that night at Sohel's party—the night they'd done nothing but tease and play and kiss. The warmth in her face spread through her body. He hadn't lost his touch, nor had she lost the urge to gravitate toward him. Her brain had shut down, though. She couldn't think of a dang thing to say.

In a low voice, Jonah asked. "You got your salon space. Is there anything else you're wishing for? Something an elf could handle?"

Kalpani could barely breathe. If the elf was him? A kiss, a touch…more. So much more of this.

Finally, she wrenched her gaze away and sucked air into her lungs and reason back into her mind. Flirting with Jonah was not a good idea. Tumbling head over heels—or even into bed—with him was a terrible idea. He'd only be in the way of her goals. It would not end well. She knew exactly what was—and wasn't—in her future.

"I have everything I need now." She glanced at him and caught a flash of something cross his face. Hurt? Anger? Frustration?

Disappointment lodged in her chest, but it didn't

matter. She was here on business, and business it would remain until he was out of her building and out of her life.

———

The holiday passed in a blur, but Kalpani had a bit of breathing room between Christmas and New Year's and was determined to see Meenu. She'd told Meenu she wouldn't take no for an answer—she had gifts for her children—and they agreed on Monday. Not only was it Kalpani's day off, she hoped Meenu's husband would be at work.

When Kalpani pulled up to the town house, there was no car in the drive. She parked on the street, just in case, wrestled the big tote of presents, and rang the bell.

Meenu opened the door wearing a smile on her face and baby Sunny on her hip. Meenu was never at ease these days, but didn't seem too stiff or agitated, and Kalpani breathed a sigh of relief. Her husband must not be home.

Her two other kiddos clamored around, excited by the peek of colorful Christmas wrapping they could see sticking out of her bag.

"It's so good to see you," Kalpani said, hugging her friend. She tickled the kids' bellies. "And you two! When did you grow up on me?"

They giggled.

"Gifts first?" Kalpani asked. Maybe if the kids were occupied with new toys, she and Meenu could manage a decent chat.

"Sure," Meenu said. "Everybody to the living room."

Kalpani passed out gifts, the kids tore into them, and Meenu made sure they each said their thank yous. Meenu helped the kids get the toys out of the boxes, so Kalpani ended up with the baby. She was a warm, solid weight, and although Kalpani made silly faces, she felt a pang deep inside. With the goals she'd set out, she didn't know how she'd manage to have kids herself.

But this visit wasn't about her. Meenu's kids seemed to be happy—typical children—so far. But Kalpani worried about the long term for this little clan, and she was especially concerned about her friend.

When Meenu judged them occupied enough, she invited Kalpani to the kitchen for tea. Kalpani noticed her friend walked gingerly.

"Are you limping?"

"Oh, I pulled something when I was running with the jogging stroller."

Kalpani found that suspicious. She'd already gathered that Meenu didn't leave her husband in charge of the kids if at all possible, and it'd be next to impossible to push three children up even a small Pittsburgh hill walking, let alone running.

Meenu didn't look at her, just popped the baby in a highchair, put a handful of Cheerios in a bright plastic cup with a tricky lid, and pushed the lever on the electric tea kettle. She already had two mugs and tea bags out.

Kalpani suspected Meenu wanted her in and out as quickly as possible. "Is Doug at work?"

"Returning some gifts at a couple of places."

Kalpani nodded. For Meenu's sake she wouldn't linger, but she wasn't leaving until she'd said what she needed to either.

They made idle chitchat, asking about each other's parents and siblings. As soon as the tea was ready and

Meenu sat, however, Kalpani said, "I have a gift for you, too."

"What? We promised to stop exchanging years ago."

"I know. This is different." Kalpani wasn't sure where to start. "Let me tell you my good news first. I am the proud owner of a new salon."

"Oh, Kalpani! You did it!" Meenu said. Her facial expression was, for once, uncensored and showed true joy. "Did you name it Xanadu like you always wanted?"

Kalpani grinned. "Yes. Renovations start end of this week." She kept it brief, explaining about the Gupta family and the excellent location. Although she would have loved to dish about Jonah with her old friend—she thought about him far more than she probably should—she was determined to stay on topic.

"That sounds amazing. I'm so happy for you," Meenu said.

"Thanks." Kalpani spun her mug, not sure how to frame the next part. "So, here's where you come in. I'm going to need an accountant."

Right off, Meenu began shaking her head. "No. I couldn't. I'm needed here." She pushed up from the table, and her chair fell over with a bang. The baby began crying, and she scooped her up. The older two ran in. "Mommy's okay. It's just my chair. See?"

Kalpani swallowed hard. These kids were not unscathed, as she had hoped. She hurried around the other side of the table and righted the chair. "There, all better." She only wished everything could be solved as easily.

The kids looked to Meenu. She nodded. "Go play now." She scooped up the mugs in one hand and put them in the sink.

"Meenu," Kalpani said.

Meenu worked one-handed. Tea bags into the sink, mugs into the dishwasher.

"Look at me," Kalpani said. "I'm not saying now. And I'm not pushing you."

Tears filled Meenu's eyes, but she didn't respond or even move until the baby yanked hard on her hair, and she automatically worked the chubby fist loose. Meenu had never confided the details of her marriage, but she had to know that Kalpani had a pretty good idea of what she was dealing with.

"I hope and pray you'll find the strength you need… someday." As much as Kalpani wanted that day to be today, there was only one person who could make that happen. All Kalpani could do was give her friend a lifeline to grab when she was ready. "When you do, you'll have a job. That's all."

**8**

———————

Jonah thought of Kalpani often in the following weeks. Who was he kidding? He thought of her constantly. He knew she was a Christian Indian and wondered what her Christmas celebrations might be like in her family. He wondered if she was extra busy at work—making people beautiful for holiday gatherings—or if it slowed down. He wondered how often she'd come to check on the renovation once it started and when—or if—he might see her again.

His own holiday was somber and bittersweet. He declined invitations from pals for holiday gatherings. He wasn't in the mood and didn't want to waste a minute of the two weeks he had left in the shop. He'd been working on a special gift for his mom and brothers, converting a snapshot taken at a barbecue the summer before his dad's death into a signature-style JW piece. In it, his mom was in front of his dad, his arm over her chest, hand on her opposite shoulder—with the spatula he held precariously close to Jonah's cheek. Chuck, wearing his ever-present bandana, was saying something into Rita's ear but looking at the camera, and her face showed mock outrage though her eyes were bright. All the men were lined up, arms linked over each other's shoulders. Jake was grinning, Jonah was rolling his eyes, and Jeremy was smirking.

When they opened his gift, everyone loved it. His mom sobbed, Sadie sniffed and swiped, and his bothers choked up. Even Jeremy's fiancée Darcy—they were suddenly back together and furiously happy—got weepy.

"Wow. This is… Damn," Jake said.

Jeremy managed, "Thanks." But Jonah could clearly see how much it meant to each of them.

As always, they ate too much and probably drank too much, but the lively atmosphere was forced. They were all very aware that this was the first Christmas without their patriarch.

And for Jonah, double whammy. He'd only just lost his other father figure, too. His gift to himself was spending time on another piece—a shot of just him and Sohel. A customer had snapped it randomly one day then sent it to them—but it happened to be a great shot. A real day in the life. Jonah didn't have his own wall to hang it on yet. But when he did, it'd have a prime spot.

There wasn't much time, so there wasn't much choice. Other than Christmas Eve and Christmas morning with his family, Jonah worked his tail off alternately tackling Sohel's forty-some years of clutter and attacking the list of things he needed to do in order to sell art.

He worked furiously to print up and gallery-wrap extra copies of his bestselling pieces and secured two local businesses to consign in after the holidays. For now, he could still use the Print & Ship's windows. Once he'd let the customers know they were closed for business, he changed over the whole second window to display his *holidays in the 'burgh pieces*, and people were actually buying them. On Saturday, he'd done nothing but handle art sales— hallelujah. The extra income would likely cover a security deposit for an apartment—not that he'd had time to look yet.

The website was a far more time-consuming project than he'd expected, and although it needed more work and a lot more real-time content, it was now at least a working site that showcased a lot of his pieces. He had yet to set up automating sales and accepting payments online, but the contact page worked. People could reach out and inquire and order through him over email or phone.

With the website address secured, he was able to complete simple flyers and business cards and print stacks of each.

And then his time was up. He had to move out, and the equipment had to be moved upstairs. He called his brothers and enlisted their help.

New Year's Eve morning, Jake showed up with breakfast sandwiches and Jeremy brought giant Bloody Marys.

"To Sohel and your last night under this roof," Jeremy said, raising his glass.

"To new beginnings," Jake added, and they touched their plastic tumblers together.

Jeremy would move into his mom's spare room tomorrow, on New Year's Day. Tonight, he wanted to spend alone, in Sohel's space. One last night with the spirit of the man who'd been so good to him, who'd meant so much.

"Speaking of new beginnings," Jeremy said, "we picked a date."

"To pick your noses?" Jonah asked.

"To get married, asswipe."

Jonah laughed. "I just like to hear you say it."

"Never thought we would," Jake said with a grin.

"Can you stop being idiots for a minute?" Jeremy said. "It's going to be a small wedding in True Springs, so we aren't going crazy, but I'd like you both to stand up for me. Best men."

"We'd be honored," Jonah said, at the same time Jake said, "Of course."

They did the man-hug-back-slap thing and then toasted again to Jeremy and Darcy's happiness.

"Who are the bridesmaids? Does Darcy have sisters?" Jake asked.

"The sister-in-law she was closest with passed, so she's going to ask Sadie." He turned from Jake to Jonah. "Her best friend, Kalpani, will be the other one. Sorry, dude."

Jonah shrugged. "It's cool." Hell, he thought about her so often that seeing her couldn't possibly make it worse. "We're on decent terms." They'd worked out a deal they could both live with. Nice and businesslike.

Jake waved his arm around. "Still kinda sucks." One night when he was feeling low, Jonah had let slip how bad he had it for Kalpani, but it seemed Jeremy hadn't shared that nugget with Jake. Jonah could only hope Jeremy hadn't spilled to Darcy either. Best if no one knew and Jeremy forgot. Maybe Jonah could forget.

Jonah said, "Yeah, but it's not her fault."

Jeremy told them the wedding date—Saturday, February fifteenth—and they discussed a few more details. When they'd finished their Bloody Marys, Jonah said, "We should get a move on."

They spent the next few hours hauling all the equipment Jonah had decided to keep—with Ranji's blessing—upstairs. The wide-format printer was a bitch, and for a while there Jonah thought they might have to start Kalpani's demo a little early, but in the end, they managed it.

The second floor was divided in three parts. Besides the bathroom, the area in the middle was just wide-open space, and they stacked boxes of valuable supplies like cardstock ink and more there, shoving them under the big table Jonah used for making stretcher frames and gallery-wrapping the art. He left the lumber in the corner. Jonah had cleared the rear storage room out and had set up a table so that the electronics wouldn't be on the dusty floor. They packed it tight.

The front room was the room he'd been using as a bedroom. He'd already cleaned out and packed up. The dresser, nightstand, and bedframe were from his childhood room. Rita didn't want them back, so a service was coming to pick them up for donation the next day. When he got his own place, he wanted to start fresh. No more twin bed for a guy who was six feet. It was past time to start adulting.

"I owe you," Jonah told his brothers when they'd finished.

"Bet your ass you do," Jeremy said, even as Jake said, "It's all good."

"Sadie and I are going to Vine tonight. Join us," Jake said.

"Dog Daze is playing," Jeremy said. "It'll be packed."

Jonah declined, and they pushed harder. Finally, with a worried look, Jake said, "Dude, are you sure?"

"I'm good," Jonah replied. "Seriously. I'm taking Mom to a nice dinner downtown, and then I'll just chill."

With the calendar ushering in a new year, Jonah was feeling contemplative. Hell—he was missing his father, missing Sohel, missing everything that had been, and although he fought against it, he was even missing Kalpani. She'd popped back into his life, and he kept wondering what could have been, if only they didn't have opposite interests.

And he could only imagine what it felt like to his mom. She'd been with his father longer than Jonah had been alive, and unlike couples who went their separate ways during the day, his parents had even been united in their work.

Jonah knew his mom counted herself blessed. They'd had a great marriage, faced tough times head-on together, had always put family first, and had been each other's go-to for so many years—but damn, it had to be hard on the other side. And New Year's Eve was another "first" without his dad for her.

So no, Jonah wasn't hanging out at Vine—something he could do anytime—or hitting some crowded, ear-splitting New Year's Eve spectacular with friends. His unknown future would be toasted, sure. Otherwise, he and his mom would quietly celebrate the past.

**9**

_______

*Three weeks later*
*Wednesday, January 21st*

Thursday nights were late ones at the downtown salon—later tonight due to a late and very particular client. Add in a stop at the market and a quick dinner, and Kalpani didn't arrive in the Strip and enter Xanadu until after ten p.m. It had been a long day and a long week, and she wondered if she shouldn't have waited to check on things until the weekend.

Her exhaustion vanished, however, as she crossed into the front room.

Lou and his subs had put up Sheetrock—and suddenly the place looked less like a torn-apart Print & Ship and more like it would be her Xanadu.

Giant boxes—the cabinets—took up a huge amount of room on the first floor. She walked through them, trailing a hand over the top. Someone had ripped a few open—likely to check that it was the correct delivery.

"Wow," she said quietly, thrilled at seeing her choice for real.

A clatter sounded from above, and she froze. What the hell?

She waited for more, but it was quiet. Just as she'd decided maybe something the contractors had propped up had fallen over, more noise came. A scrabbling sound or…

She didn't know. Dammit. Had the Sheetrock guys left a window open, maybe? Had a bird gotten in?

There was a push broom in one corner, and she grabbed it and headed for the back stairs. It wasn't ideal for shooing out a bird, but her options were limited.

She crept up the stairs. Any rodent or bird would panic at the approach of a human, and she was hoping to sneak up on a calm thing, not a crazed one.

She heard only a bit of noise a couple of times. Mostly it was quiet.

When she hit the landing, she realized there was light. They must have left lights on, too, but at least she'd be able to see.

Kalpani crept forward, scanning around that big table Jonah had left and all the boxes under it. If she were a squirrel, she'd hide in there. The area to her left at the front of the building had been gutted, updated, and Sheetrocked like the first floor. New windows were in place, but from here didn't appear to be open. If she were a bird, she'd be aiming for a window.

She swore under her breath when she turned toward the back of the building and realized light spilled from the back room. Lou hadn't kept the door to Jonah's storage space closed like she'd told them to. His stuff was probably covered in dust and grime.

She listened hard for noise, heard nothing as she crept to within a few feet of the door, then suddenly a creak and a shadow dipped in and out of the light. She took a big breath and covered the remaining distance, broom held high, ready to swing if the thing should attack.

Then—

A huge shape rose up, blocking the light. She screamed.

"Ho-whoa!"

Kalpani couldn't see the face, hidden in the shadow. Her brain processed like lightning—if this was an intruder, she should strike first, then run for it. If it was the contractor or a sub or Jonah—

She knew that voice. "Jonah?"

"Kalpani, what the hell are you doing?"

"Me? What the hell are *you* doing? You scared me to death."

"And what—that broom was going to make up for your five-foot height and you were going to fend off an intruder?" Jonah spun away, then turned back to her, face no longer in shadow, and she saw he was furious. "You shouldn't have come up here armed. You should have called the cops and left the building. Don't *ever* put yourself in that situation."

"Don't *you* put me in that situation. And for your information, I didn't think I was confronting a person. I thought I was going to be chasing off a possum or something." She was pissed off because he'd scared her—and angry that she was ridiculously glad to see him. She threw the broom out into the other room, and it hit the floor with a bang.

"Down here in the Strip?" His hands went to his hips.

"I don't know—a raccoon or a bird. I thought maybe a

window had been left open. And then I thought— Never mind." Kalpani huffed out a breath. "What the hell are you doing here, anyway?"

"I—" He waved a hand and shook his head. "I realized I needed something—some files from the hard drive."

The screen was on and his laptop appeared to be on as well. It sat open on bit of table that wasn't covered in boxes or printers.

"You couldn't have come in the daytime like a normal person?"

He rolled his eyes. "It seemed easier to just come tonight and not be in anyone's way."

There were stacks of paper beside him, and she leaned forward to look.

"I decided to take some stuff I had boxed up, too. Since I was already here." He shifted slightly, blocking her view. "I'll just get what I need and get out of here. If you'll give me a minute."

"Fine."

Kalpani stalked out of the room, snatched up the broom, and stomped back down the stairs. Once she put the broom back where she found it, she pushed her hair out of her face and looked around, at a loss and unreasonably off balance. She'd told him he could store his stuff up there, but she'd assumed he'd access it during the day, not sneak in at night. He'd scared the daylights out of her, and anger was a side effect of being scared. Annoyance was a side effect of the oddly joyous feeling that had leapt in her chest at seeing him.

He looked like shit, frankly. His brown hair was too long, his dark scruff bordered on a beard, there were unhealthy circles under his eyes—yet still, he looked so dang good.

She heard his footsteps above and shook her head. She told herself she couldn't leave him here alone, but really, the urge to see him again—without a makeshift weapon in hand—rooted her in place. She'd missed him these last few weeks. Before the holidays, she'd gotten used to popping in to deliver him news every few days. But after? She didn't even know where he was living until Darcy told her.

She had recognized his art in two other shop windows and wondered how he was faring. People should be buying it. His work was unique and compelling and should appeal to anybody who loved Pittsburgh.

She hadn't expected to bump into him until Darcy's wedding, so tonight was—

Well, dang. It was more exciting than it should be.

Which wasn't good. Perhaps he wasn't exactly rabid with sharp teeth or a beak—but he was a danger to her nonetheless. Instinctively she knew that if she let Jonah close, he wouldn't be easy to shake. And she simply didn't want or need the complication of a man in her life. Never would.

---

Jonah hit save, transferred the file he'd been working on, and powered down the printers. He grabbed a box and shoved in the postcards he'd made and the new stickers he'd printed to adhere to the back of all his art.

He swore under his breath the whole time. He'd gotten too comfortable, too complacent. A few weeks ago, he had received his first order on Etsy—at which point he'd realized he had left all the packing and shipping supplies at the shop. The next time he'd slipped in after hours, it was because he'd needed some files stored only on the hard drive. Then one night he'd been desperate to use the canvas printer to start restocking what had become skimpy displays post-holidays at the shops he'd been consigning with. Working at his mom's was unproductive and extremely limited, and the next thing he knew, he'd practically reversed his schedule, working most nights for at least a few hours in secret in the storage room that he had no rights to.

He knew damn well that he should have begged Kalpani to ask her contractor if it was okay, since the renovation was further along. But he didn't want to risk being told no. The ability to access his equipment was too damn tempting. Hell, it was necessary. How could he make enough of a living to commit to one of these overpriced studio spaces if he couldn't even produce?

Jonah snatched up his laptop and powered down the computer. He looked around. What else did he need if he wasn't coming back?

He didn't think Kalpani had noticed, but he'd blocked the window with a big piece of cardboard. He didn't want some well-meaning neighbor to call the police or even Kalpani's contractor. He pulled it down and stuck it behind a bunch of stacked items. Jonah was about to hit the switch when he saw his thermos of coffee. He grabbed it and shoved it down into the box. Kalpani could be downstairs right now putting two and two together, and he didn't want to give her any more ammunition than necessary.

*Kalpani*—both a welcome and unwelcome sight. He

desperately wished she hadn't caught him here—he had so much work still to do—and yet, damn, was she something, a tiny sprite raising that broom like a warrior woman.

Jonah headed down the stairs with his box. Kalpani stood, arms crossed over her front, in the middle of the main room.

"Sorry about scaring you," he said.

"Sorry about nearly maiming you."

He raised an eyebrow.

"You doubt me? Those bristles would have done some damage."

"You, I would never doubt." He chuckled. "I'm pretty sure you'll succeed at anything you put your mind to, including maiming."

She ducked her head.

"I'm serious. Look at this place." He waved his free arm. "It's your dream, coming to life."

She looked up at him and smiled. "It is, isn't it?"

His heart actually skipped a beat.

"Want to see my cabinets?"

He set his box on the floor. "Sure." He wanted to see anything she wanted to show him, to stay in her presence as long as possible.

She walked around some waist-high boxes, and he followed. She waved her hand with a flourish at one with the wrapping spread open.

"Nice." He was standing so close that he could smell her. Something citrusy and a slight chemical scent. She'd come from work, he was sure. "What color are you doing the walls?"

"Gray. Purple and red accents. Tire-tread metal kick plates in front of each stylist's station. Mirrors above, of course. It needs to look hip and cool, but also a little rich and lush."

He smiled. "I can see it. Good choices."

"I hope so." She smoothed one hand over the back of the other and then reversed the action. "It's all ordered. No going back now."

He turned to her. "No need. You're on your way." The urge to reach for her, reassure her with his touch, was nearly overpowering.

"What about you? I saw your art in a couple of windows."

Jonah drew a tight breath. She was so short that whenever she spoke to him, it seemed like she was tilting her lips up as an offering. "A fair amount of the holiday art sold, which is cool. But consigning sucks."

Now it was her turn to raise her eyebrows.

He shrugged. "They take a cut and I don't get that much space. Had to raise my prices to compensate. And, of course, post-holiday sales are down."

"I guess that's no surprise," she said. "But your stuff is really cool. I can see both locals and visitors buying it."

He nodded. "That's true, given the people that used to come in off the street to ask about it."

"You'll get there," she said. She looked like she wanted to say more but didn't.

"I'm trying." They still stood face to face, only about a foot apart. Too close for strangers, too far for a man and a woman who had shared kisses and a magical night under the stars.

Even now, the air felt charged. Jonah was sure she felt it too—her eyes practically reached for him.

"So…" She pulled her hair over one shoulder. "I guess I'll be seeing you at the wedding."

"Yeah, good news, right?"

"The best," she said. "I'm glad they came out the other side of that mess."

"Me too," he said. "They seem…meant to be."

"I hope so," she said, but a shadow crossed her face.

He frowned. "You aren't worried, are you? Jeremy's a good guy—the best."

She shook her head. "No, it's just— Nothing. I'm sure those two will be very happy. Darcy already is."

"Jeremy, too." He bent and grabbed his box. "I'd better go."

"I should, too," she said. They walked toward the back, and she flipped the lights off behind them.

"You want me to walk you to your car? Since you aren't taking the broom?"

She smiled. "I'm right out back."

They stepped out into the night, and both got out their keys to lock the back door. Jonah bowed slightly and stepped back. It was Kalpani's to lock up. He shouldn't even still have a key, but he shoved it back in his pocket anyway.

He looked up between the buildings at the night sky.

Kalpani stood shoulder to shoulder with him. "It's quiet down here tonight."

"Surprising for a Thursday." His voice was tight, and he realized he was struggling not to express any emotion. But inside? He was a mess of them. It felt like he wasn't only losing the space but losing the connection with Sohel. And he longed to haul the new owner into his arms and kiss her for all he was worth.

Maybe that showed in his eyes, because she looked up at him—those lips—and then away quickly. She hit a button on her key fob and lights flashed from her car. She walked away, waving over her shoulder.

"See you in True Springs," she said.

"See you in True Springs," he said softly.

A whole weekend of seeing Kalpani was something to look forward to. Not all was lost.

**10**

———————

*Two weeks later*
*Saturday, February 8th*

Kalpani would meet Darcy later for the usual Saturday yoga and breakfast, then she had a full day of clients, but the first order of business was Xanadu. She wanted to check on the progress and arrived bright and early. She let herself in the back door, then set her coffee on the counter. *Her* counters.

She smiled and spun around, taking it all in. The floors were in, and the cabinets and counters and reception desk had all been installed, right along with the sinks where they'd shampoo hair or rinse out color.

The chairs were next. Kalpani couldn't help the big grin that she wore—*her* salon was actually looking like a salon now instead of a shell of a space.

She headed up the back stairs, wondering if they'd completed the flooring up there as well. The contractor had mentioned he'd need to move Jonah's things, and she hoped he'd been considerate and not dumped them haphazardly.

As soon as she reached the top, she saw light spilling from Jonah's storage room.

She narrowed her eyes and crept forward. Had Jonah snuck in again?

She peeked cautiously around the doorway—expecting him to jump up and scare her again, even though this time she was prepared. But no.

Jonah was head down, arm pillowing his head, fast asleep. She could hear him breathing deeply. He was still overly scruffy, but wow was he beautiful. The hard cheekbones and strong nose were still there, but the fan of dark lashes and the relaxed lips softened the whole.

She put her hands on her hips and shook her head—annoyed that she had such a strong urge to touch him, upset that he'd used a key he shouldn't have—again. He no longer lived here or worked here. The building had a new owner, for goodness' sake—*her*. And her contractor had expressly said he hadn't wanted the liability of anyone in the building. Jonah knew that.

She felt herself getting worked up, and she glared at his sleeping form.

A stack of business cards caught her eye. She could read them from here: a website address, an Etsy address. There were flyers, too—a gallery show downtown—featuring Jonah along with a few other artists.

Good for him. The big screen on the desk was lit up, and she moved into the room a little further to see what was on it. It was blown up big and she couldn't see it all, but bold colors—purples and reds—flowed into a swirl. It was stunning.

Kalpani frowned. On the desk was an open laptop, an insulated to-go mug, and a pack of cinnamon gum. Jonah hadn't budged, not even a change of breathing, since she'd walked in here. The man was exhausted.

And it hit her—he hadn't just snuck in tonight. He'd totally disregarded her contractor's wishes not just once or twice. This was a regular thing…

Because he needed these machines, because he was working hard to create and sell art through the setback of losing his storefront display and workspace.

Kalpani winced, and the anger that had been building inside her dissipated as quickly as if she'd popped a balloon.

Of all people, Kalpani understood pushing toward a dream and working hard toward future goals. She respected someone who forged ahead despite obstacles— even harder when there were obstacles, finding a path around them. Hell, hadn't she done the very same in securing this building for herself?

Kalpani took a deep breath and slowly exhaled.

She could only assume he hadn't meant to fall asleep, that he'd meant to leave as secretly as he came well before sunrise. Ever so quietly, she reached into her bag and pulled out the granola bar and banana she'd brought to get her through hot yoga. The power bar's wrapper crinkled loudly, and she froze, but Jonah didn't even flinch.

Carefully, she placed them on the desk next to Jonah's elbow. She reached to smooth back his hair but snatched her hand back just in time. *What is with me?* she wondered, as she crept out of the room and downstairs.

She wasn't sure if the contractor or his subs would be in this morning, but she'd call Lou from her car. Surely the renovation was no longer dangerous. If he was okay with it, she'd let Lou know she'd like for Jonah to be able to come and go. She might as well take the pressure off, since this surely wouldn't be the last time he snuck in.

She left her purse on the counter, trading it for her coffee cup, then moved to the front windows, which were taped over with brown paper. There was a tear, and she watched as the Strip began to come alive. A dad with two small children in a stroller walked past, likely to one of the diners, maybe letting Mom sleep in. A couple walked past with reusable shopping bags. They'd probably hit the fish or meat markets before the crowds descended and then get breakfast. The oversized metal door of a business across Penn Ave rose with a rush of noise, and another owner twisted a key in the lock and shouldered her door open.

Kalpani couldn't wait to be a part of this community and open her own doors to clients.

She looked at the ceiling and took another deep breath. New doors were on order for the salon, but for now she found herself strangely glad that Jonah's key still worked. Losing the shop had to have set him back, and she wanted to help him succeed.

She shook her head at herself. What was it about Jonah that made her say yes, when she should be saying no?

## 11



*Nearly one week later*
*Friday February 14th, Valentine's Day*

Jonah hadn't expected to see Kalpani again until he arrived in True Springs—but there she was standing on the side of the highway, phone pressed to her ear with one hand, the other on her hip, and her hair blowing wildly despite her knit cap. She always looked like a woman who could take on the world—but apparently, she couldn't solve smoke pouring out of her little SUV's hood.

Jonah quickly moved into the right lane, then slowed enough to pull off the highway. Carefully, he reversed.

Kalpani spotted his car and moved to the rear of hers. She crossed her arms, even as she remained on the phone. She'd never seen his vehicle and assumed he was a total stranger. He should probably be glad she was holding her phone and not another broom.

He climbed out and waved even as he pulled on his winter jacket. She looked wary—as she should. There were no houses in sight, and he'd guess they were at least ten miles to an exit in either direction.

He saw her relax as soon as he got close enough for her to realize who he was.

"Trouble, huh?"

"Obviously." She threw out her hands. Then she shook her head. "Sorry, I'm just so flipping annoyed. I just had it serviced. And I was nearly there. This couldn't have waited?"

She was right—True Springs was only another couple of exits. "Did you call AAA?"

She heaved out a big breath. "I called a while ago. They should be here in about ten minutes. I don't suppose you are handy with cars?"

"Only if you need a flat tire changed. Or maybe"—he tilted his head—"if you wanted some cool design for detailing."

She shook her head, too miserable to even crack a smile. He walked to his car, opened the passenger side door, and retrieved his own winter hat and two bottles of water. It was cold here on the side of the highway with the cars rushing past, upping the wind factor.

He handed her a water bottle, then gestured to the guardrail about eight feet away. "How about we get off the berm?"

She followed him. When he got comfortable against the rail, legs extended and crossed in front of him, she said, "You don't have to stay with me."

He shrugged and drank from his water bottle.

"Seriously," she said, "I'm sure your brother is expecting you."

"There's no way I'm leaving you here alone, and

Jeremy would have my hide if I left his fiancée's lovely friend stranded on the highway in the middle of nowhere. Darcy, too, for that matter."

"Fine. Have it your way."

Jonah smiled at her crossness. Kalpani was like a cornered cat. Knowing she was stuck but taking her swipes anyway, just in case you decided she was easy prey.

Obviously solo kitty was not in the mood for conversation, so he just watched the cars zoom by, watched the grasses sway in the wind. His mind wandered and he couldn't help thinking that if he'd really had it his way, they'd have been driving to the wedding together in the first place with the promise of celebrating a wedding on Valentine's Day weekend in a quaint little town that was known for romance.

He glanced sideways at her tight expression. Yeah, he'd have to remain content with making sure she got there safely.

The AAA representative arrived, asked Kalpani some questions, and poked around under the car's hood. When he pronounced it not fixable without parts, Kalpani swore. After a few more questions and answers, they sorted that the car would be towed all the way to True Springs to a guy named Mac who could supposedly fix anything.

While the man was prepping her car for the tow, Kalpani approached Jonah. "Thanks for hanging here with me."

Jonah raised an eyebrow.

"He said that I can ride with him up front, so you're off the hook."

Jonah laughed. "Don't be ridiculous. Ride with me."

She shook her head. "It's fine, he—"

"You'd rather ride with a complete stranger than me?" Jonah said, an edge coming into his voice.

"No, it's just—" She shook her head. "I don't want to owe you anything."

"You don't owe me a thing. If anything, I owe you." She opened her mouth, but he didn't want to hear it. "Just get your stuff out of your car."

She stared at him for a moment then stalked off toward her car.

He crushed his empty water bottle and shoved it into a coat pocket. She was incomprehensible to him. She needed a ride. She knew him well enough. They were literally traveling to the same place. He swore, then went to his own car and cleared off the passenger seat, which took all of a minute.

Leaning against his trunk with his arms crossed, he waited and watched. She leaned into the Toyota's front seat, and when she backed out, her purse bulged. Then she yanked open her back door, and out came a suitcase and another tote. She had a brief conversation with the technician, who nodded before turning to winch up the car.

Jonah walked to meet her and took her bags the remaining distance to stash them in his trunk alongside his own.

When they got in, he asked, "Did you get an address for this mechanic?"

"He said we can't miss it. It's just outside of True Springs."

Jonah nodded, waited for a break in traffic, and pulled onto the highway.

She said, "Listen, it's not you. I don't like to owe anything to anyone."

"Whatever." Jonah shook his head. Did he seem like the kind of person that would ask for payment or expect an eye for an eye?

She looked out the window, then around his car. He kept his eyes on the road.

"I didn't expect to see one of these this weekend," she said. He followed her gaze, and she pointed to an intricately carved sandalwood elephant that had always perched in the console. "Did Sohel give it to you?"

"It came with the car."

"Sohel's?"

He nodded. She didn't say a word, didn't even move a muscle. However, he was already ticked off that she hadn't wanted to ride with him, and the simple question made her long-ago "freeloader" comment rush back to him. "I *bought* the car from him when it became clear he'd never drive again." He couldn't help the anger in his voice.

She raised her hands and reared back a little. "Okay."

They rode in silence the rest of the way.

———

Kalpani entered Mac's repair shop and froze. The last thing she'd expected to see in this kind of establishment was blinking neon hearts strung up along the ceiling.

A tall, lanky guy in a ball cap and coveralls came out of a door wiping his hands on a cloth. Younger and cuter than she'd pictured, but Mac it was. He saw her glance at the lights and smiled.

She said, "I forgot it was Valentine's Day."

"Those? They stay there all year long."

Her surprise must have shown on her face.

"New to True Springs?" he asked.

"Yes, I'm attending a wedding here this weekend."

"Well, then you'll get a double dose, likely."

"Of what?"

"All the town has to offer." Mac looked out the window, and his glance seemed speculative. Or maybe sympathetic? Mac was probably wondering how a woman who had a handsome guy—patiently leaning against the hood of her car—forgot it was Valentine's Day.

Jonah hadn't offered to come in with her, but she'd made it clear she didn't want any help, hadn't she?

"You need something for your vehicle?" Mac asked.

"That car is fine," Kalpani said. "My car should be arriving shortly on a tow truck."

"You're the one they called about, then." He slid behind the desk and put a pen and a printed sheet—carbon paper, of all things—on the counter. "Leave me your info, and I'll update you as soon as I know what's wrong with it."

Kalpani did, thanked him, and pushed out the door.

Jonah stood, but didn't look her in the eye.

Well, she'd been wondering how to not get drawn in by him this weekend. Seemed that problem was taking care of itself.

## 12

When they arrived in True Springs, Jonah pulled up in front of the Sweetwater Inn, where many of the guests were staying and where the rehearsal dinner would be. He got out and lifted Kalpani's bags from the trunk.

"Thanks for the ride," she said with a lame smile.

"No problem. You want help with these?" God forbid he just carried them to the door—she'd probably unsheathe the cat claws again.

She was already extending the handle on the rolling case and quickly plunked the tote on top of it. "I'm okay. Thanks."

He nodded and tore his eyes away from her retreating form. Seemed she was always running from him.

Jonah eyed the giant statue of an embracing couple above a big, round fountain across the intersection. He swore. What a crap way to start what could have been a romantic weekend.

Jonah made his way to the outskirts of town to Valeska's Inn, a funky bed and breakfast that sounded more his style. Apparently, the owner served homemade *sopapillas* —fried Mexican pastries—in the morning, and according to the online reviews, they were to die for. He had suspected he'd want a little breathing room from family and festivities. After the tense ride with Kalpani, he was doubly glad for some space.

There was plenty of time to shower and change and talk some with the owner Maribel and her man, a jazz musician named Jory. Eventually he said, "So your place seems to be one of the only places around not dripping with hearts and magic."

"Maribel marches to the beat of her own drum, man," Jory said, and his eyes crinkled up in a smile at the dark-haired beauty. It was clear they were crazy about each other.

"What's with this legend?" Jonah had seen a sign on the way into town, and there'd been a little story brochure in his room.

Maribel and Jory exchanged glances. She shrugged, but the corner of one lip turned up. "Both of us are transplants, so it's hard to say, but we think there's something to it."

Jonah's brothers seemed to prove the theory, too, but surely it didn't work for every Tom, Dick, and Jane.

Killing time, Jonah poked around the first floor. Valeska's Inn was a stately mansion with intricate moldings and old-world craftsmanship converted to bright, uncluttered, adobe-themed living. The juxtaposition appealed to him, and he was already considering how to incorporate the idea in his art.

Equilibrium restored, Jonah made his way to town. The Sweetwater Inn's small parking lot was full, but he found a spot a couple blocks further. He ambled along Main Street, eyeing the unique shops and eateries. Each venue played on the true love theme to varying degrees, and though it was overkill, Jonah did appreciate the creativity.

Since he was on foot, he crossed to the town fountain with the life-sized couple atop it. Artistically speaking, the fountain wasn't anything that amazing—but it evoked feeling, he'd give it that. The man spun the woman around, just like Jonah had spun Kalpani when she'd told him her offer on the shop had been accepted—except this couple was lip-locked. Jonah read the plaque. When they reunited after WWII, Miles Hoffman's bus ticket had fallen into the natural spring fountain at the very moment he and Adele had kissed. Ever since, the town's water was thought to be touched by magic—and drinking it would find a person's true love.

Jonah noticed the spout and laughed.

A short, slightly plump, white-haired lady leaned out the door of the General Store across the street. In a surprisingly loud voice, she yelled, "It's not a laughing matter. You'll see."

Boy, she must have some seriously powerful hearing aids. "Sorry!" He waved.

This was nuts. There was no way the water was some true-love tonic. His brothers weren't suckers. That couple, Maribel and Jory, seemed like reasonable people. It was more likely the legend—the belief, the option—simply opened a person's mind to the possibility of love.

He snorted. Well, Kalpani's mind was made up about him. If she didn't want to ride in a car with him for even forty-five minutes and believed he was the kind of guy who wouldn't help someone without asking for something in return? It was highly unlikely a little sip of True Springs's legendary water was going to change that.

But this stay wasn't about him and Kalpani. It was about Jeremy and Darcy, and he couldn't put off the rehearsal dinner any longer.

The manager of the Sweetwater Inn, Maddie Kate, a curly blond, introduced herself. She seemed to be trying not to laugh.

"What?" Jonah asked.

"So, you met Mabel."

"Is that the bullhorn's name?"

She laughed. "She takes our legend very seriously."

"No kidding."

Maddie Kate pointed out the big room where the rehearsal dinner was being held and the bar at the far end, which Jonah headed directly for. He spotted Kalpani across the room talking animatedly with someone. Far more at ease than she'd been with him today. Figured.

As it turned out, there was no rehearsing planned. The gathering was just a chance for Darcy and Jeremy's families and friends to get to know each other. While Jonah socialized, he kept a close eye on his mom, but so far, she seemed to be having a blast.

Kalpani frowned when she saw him, but Jonah approached her anyway.

So she had the wrong idea about him? So what. He was sick and tired of trying to prove anything to anyone, and he was determined to enjoy this weekend. There was already a messy mix of emotions, given that his dad wasn't here to see the second of his sons tie the knot, but it was important that they all celebrate something positive together. Smoothing things over with Kalpani would make that easier.

He enjoyed her company—had from the first moment they'd met. He'd just try to refrain from putting any pressure on that—from wishing that it could be more, from wishing she saw him differently. If something shifted and she was willing to give him a chance, he was all in. Otherwise, friendly was a decent happy medium.

"All settled in?" he asked.

She nodded, and her posture relaxed when she saw that he wasn't holding a grudge. "Freshened up, too."

"You look great. Although you always do." She looked stunning, in fact. Her shining black hair was perfectly styled and her makeup showcased her dark eyes. She wore a white top with a chunky beaded necklace and swishy black pants that, at first glance, he'd thought were a long skirt. "And taller." She had traded sneakers for heels—now she topped out at his collarbone.

"Definitely taller. A virtual giant." Her mouth twitched into a smile. "Thank you. You look nice, too."

He inclined his head. "There's a first for everything." She smiled, knowing he was joking. He wore khakis and a plaid button-down. She hadn't seen him in more than a t-shirt and jeans—lately covered in grime, too—since Sohel's long-ago birthday party.

"Speaking of firsts," he said, and raised his bottle of beer, "to new beginnings."

She raised her glass—some pink Valentine's Day concoction from the menu he'd seen on the bar—and repeated the sentiment. Then she said, "A lot of us here do have new beginnings, don't we?"

"We do." He thought about telling her how great the salon was starting to look and then thought better of it. He still didn't know if her contractor or one of his subs had left him that simple breakfast or if Kalpani herself had. Regardless, he wasn't supposed to have seen the inside of the salon lately.

He would have been happy to stand here beside her the whole night. But he forced himself to say, "I'm going to make the rounds."

"Enjoy," she said.

They would be friends for his brother's sake, but damn, if Jonah didn't want so much more from Kalpani.

———

"Honey? You with us?"

Kalpani blinked. Rita was talking to her, something about her hair. The wedding party was crammed into a small room off the back of the True Springs Chapel—because the front door entered right up to the main congregation area and pews, without even a vestibule. It was a small, adorable, open little church with lovely stained-glass windows. Kalpani thought it gorgeous in its simplicity and all the more intimate for it.

"Yes." She smiled and reached up to tuck a lock of Rita's hair back behind her ear. The woman couldn't stay still—a whole can of hairspray wouldn't have mattered. "There. Perfect."

"Thanks."

"Of course." She liked Rita Walker a lot. Talk about

salt of the earth. But she felt heat rise in her cheeks, because she'd been standing here completely lost in thoughts about the woman's youngest son.

Jonah stood a mere six feet away, looking absolutely magazine-worthy in his tux. He'd gotten his hair cut recently—she approved; his stylist had done a good job—and, of course, today he'd shaved. He looked handsome, hip, relaxed, and oh-so-kissable.

As he had every time she'd seen him—which was constantly this weekend.

Even at seven a.m. this morning on her coffee run to Valentine's Cafe. No kidding, the cafe was at the corner of Main Street and Lover's Lane, and everything was done up in shades of rose and cream—even the servers. In addition to some divine sweet treats and sandwiches, they sold bottled spring water supposedly imbued with magical true-love properties. Kalpani had just had the thought that she'd somehow walked into a silly young girl's imagination, when she bumped into guess who? Prince Jonah. Her heart did a weird little flip.

Even when she'd expected total girl time, doing wedding-party hair for Darcy, Rita, and Sadie, Jonah had been in and out with snacks for them and then taking pictures with his fancy camera. Every single time, her body had reacted with a thrill of excitement before she could tamp it down.

It had started last night at the intimate no-rehearsal-rehearsal dinner. She'd been pleased to see that Jonah had gotten over her idiocy about riding with him. She'd known there were no strings to his offer and it made complete sense, she just...well, she'd been *too much* looking forward to seeing him, and then ridiculously thrilled to see calm, steady-mannered, I-won't-abandon-you Jonah come to the rescue. Of course, her reaction made her prickly. She'd been determined to avoid him, as she didn't *want* to like him, and he would only be a complication she didn't need. Except she couldn't seem to get that through her otherwise logical head.

When he wasn't present? Her eyes and ears reached out with yearning like she was conducting some kind of search party of the heart.

There was a flutter of action in the room and, *dang it*, Kalpani realized she'd spaced out again.

Rita grabbed the arm of one of her brothers-in-law and shot a look of pure happiness at Jeremy, then headed out the door, behind the last row of pews and into the chapel's center aisle. Kalpani peeked out, and, of course, all the guests had turned to watch with shiny eyes and wobbly smiles. She felt her throat tighten up. Rita's husband, Jeremy's father, should have been on her arm, here to see his son married.

"We're up." Jake smiled at Sadie.

Kalpani and Jonah were next.

She drew a shaky breath through her tight throat at the thought of taking his strong arm, walking hip to hip, and stealing a little support from his steadiness to get through this emotional rollercoaster. Sadness, joy, and for her—an extra-heady tangle of emotions surrounding Jonah.

Kalpani watched Jake and Sadie take those first steps. Sadie was stunning in the dark plum halter-style dress. Both she and Kalpani had similar skin tones, plus the toned back and arms for it—Sadie from waitressing, Kalpani from styling hair and yoga. Right now, however, Kalpani didn't give a thought to her own appearance.

She gripped the pretty white and green bouquet so hard that it shook.

"No big deal," Jonah said softly into her ear. Goosebumps ripped from her exposed shoulder down her arm. Little did he know, she wasn't worried about the crowd. She'd reacted because it was time to touch Jonah, to stand with Jonah, to play his partner in front of an audience.

Because Jeremy hadn't wanted to choose between his brothers, Jake and Sadie would stand behind him, and Kalpani and Jonah would stand alongside Darcy. So instead of being aligned same sex, they were coupled off for everyone to see. For Kalpani, it was both thrilling and terrifying—and so silly. She'd been in numerous weddings and never been nervous. Today, however, her heart was racing, and her nerves were on high alert.

He held out his arm. She grasped his bicep lightly and looked up at him. His green eyes sparkled. "I'll protect you."

She ripped her gaze away and lurched forward. He matched his steps to hers.

"Smile," he whispered.

"Right," she said. *And breathe.*

The ceremony was simple and short, yet so real, so heartfelt, so emotional that she was sure there wasn't a dry eye in the house.

After the vows, Jonah reached around her and handed her his handkerchief. She gulped. Hot as sin *and* thoughtful.

This wedding—Darcy and Jeremy's obvious devotion and happiness? Well, it made a girl long for things she'd swore she'd never risk and never choose.

And Jonah caring for her with his solid, reassuring

presence? Standing so close she could feel his heat? So near all she could smell was him—warm male, crisp starch, and a hint of cinnamon swirling among a classic aftershave?

It made her want to throw caution to the wind.

## 13

A whole slew of beautiful children—Darcy's many nieces and nephews—dashed on and off the dance floor created at Valeska's Inn, although in the way of young ones never in a straight line. That didn't stop the adults, however, and Jonah found himself dancing alongside Kalpani. He'd been seated with her, of course, and basically, since they'd walked down the aisle together, he felt like they'd been on a date. A very long, very fun date.

The reception celebration was lively all the way through with numerous toasts, flowing alcohol, delicious food, and the music—wow. The music was killer. Of course, Jeremy being Jeremy had picked this venue in large part because of Jory's amazing talent and the vibe he would provide. Jonah would bet anything that Jeremy had already asked him to come play at Vine.

The group Jonah and Kalpani had been dancing with retired one by one, a slow song came on, and next thing he knew, she was pressed against him.

Had he reached for her or had she come to him? He

wasn't sure who had moved first; he only knew it felt mutual. He also knew their pelvis-to-thigh, lips-to-neck, hands-in-hair routine was getting waaaay too hot for this scene. "We're pushing the limits here," he said in her ear.

"I don't care," she said.

He was gratified to see that her eyes were heavy-lidded. As always, her lips beckoned as she looked up at him.

"Almost," she said, and pushed back enough that air flowed between them. "I almost don't care."

He smiled. "How about another drink? Or some water?"

She nodded. He looped an arm around her waist and escorted her off the dance floor and to the room where there was a small bar set up.

The celebration was winding down. Many of the older folks had already retired, and the bride and groom were sitting with Jake and Sadie and some cousins.

Jonah and Kalpani both requested water, as they'd had plenty of alcohol.

"Want to get a little air?" He held out his hand.

She slipped her hand in his and let him lead her to the back of the inn. The room was largely windows and looked out over the yard and a garden he was sure would be spectacular in spring. It was hemmed in by hedges, and he wished this were like Sohel's party—warm enough weather to go out and kiss madly behind a tree again.

"What a beautiful night," Kalpani murmured.

He nodded. She looked so gorgeous in the moonlight that he didn't trust himself to speak.

Kalpani looked at him over the rim of the glass as she

drank some water, and her big eyes still held plenty of heat.

"You know what they say about the water in this town," Jonah said with a teasing smile.

"Mmm," she said. "I've heard some rumors."

"Both my brothers believe there's something to it."

"Darcy, too."

"And look at them now."

"It's ridiculous, though. A bunch of nonsense."

He laughed. "You're right," he said. "I mean, look"—he took a big gulp then raised his free hand—"nothing."

She laughed. "Are you issuing a challenge, Walker?"

"Me? Never."

She raised an eyebrow, tilted her glass, and downed the rest of the crisp liquid. She titled her head side to side. "Nothing."

"Because you don't believe."

"Don't tell me you do?"

"I believe in happy endings. But not magic."

A shadow crossed her face but was gone so fast that he thought maybe he hadn't seen it after all. She smiled and took a step toward him. "And here I thought you thought that drinking the water would make me tumble right into your arms."

"Nah," he said, "I was hoping for that long before the water."

Her eyes were pools of rich brown as they locked on his, and she took another step forward. Jonah's whole body was taut with expectation, strung with longing as soul-deep as that jazzman's notes.

She was close enough now to need to tilt her head up, and Jonah's eyes locked on her mouth.

"You have no idea how badly I want to kiss you," he said quietly, and pressed his thumb against her soft lower lip.

"Actually, I do," she whispered.

He grasped her hips, she reached for his face, their mouths fused—and his brain exploded with pleasure. She tasted like bliss, felt like perfection against him, and he couldn't help but pull her even closer.

In this moment, this was everything he wanted and needed—and yet not nearly enough. He ground against her and then forced himself to stop. She whimpered into the kiss, pushing her pelvis hard against him.

He dropped his lips to her neck. "Not here," he said, and was shocked to hear how ragged his voice sounded.

"Your room," she said.

He raised his head and pulled back enough to look her in the eye.

"I'm dead serious," she said.

*Ho-whoa.* He grabbed her hand, and they got all the way to the bar before he halted—a semblance of reason sinking into his head.

"Should we say good night, pretend maybe we…?" He shrugged. He wasn't that coherent.

"Let's just go," she said.

He glanced into the main room. He didn't see his mom, and Jake's back was to him. Jeremy, however, caught his eye and flicked his hand in the direction of the stairs.

Jonah didn't have to be told twice. He spun and tugged Kalpani along with him. Under her breath, she murmured, *"Waheguru."* Wonderful God. If she hadn't been at risk of tripping in the long bridesmaid dress, Jonah would have taken the stairs two or three at a time.

At the end of the hall, he pushed inside his room and locked the door behind him. This was a small bed-and-breakfast-type place and they knew all the other guests. "We're going to have to be quieter than I'd like to be." He put a hand behind her neck and leaned in to kiss her, but she straightened an arm and pushed against his chest.

"Wait, I have some rules, too."

He slid his hand over her shoulder, down her arms, and covered her hand with both of his on his chest. "Okay."

She took a deep breath. "One night only. It goes no further."

"Why?"

"I don't believe in happy endings, remember?"

"That is a sad, sad way to live, Kalpani Desai."

"I just want this"—she waved between them—"to have its happy culmination. I don't want to be tied down by anyone. Not now, not later, not ever. So you have to accept that and agree—or I walk away right now. Because I don't want any pressure or some big, messy extraction. No *tamasha*."

No drama, he knew she meant. "You're talking to the king of laid-back, remember?"

"That look in your eyes is the farthest thing from chill," she said.

He tried to tamp down the attraction he felt for her, but it was impossible. He'd wanted her since the moment he saw her at Sohel's party so long ago. That urge had only grown as he'd gotten to know her. She was challenging and sexy and gorgeous and amazing. He couldn't turn it off. "Sorry, but that's how badly I want you."

Her elbow bent, and he felt the rush of her breath against his neck. The tingle traveled down his spine.

"I want you, too. Badly," she said. "I want a happy ending to this physical need I ache with. But that's all it can be. Just phenomenal sex. No stupid water or sappy wedding is going to change that. One night only—and then we walk away."

Jonah's thoughts fired double-time.

*Sex so fucking phenomenal she might just want more of it.*

*Water that the populations of True Springs—and my brothers—swear helps true love along.*

*A romantic wedding, a private room, a whole night...*

"Are you in or out?"

She looked up at him and—that mouth. He put his thumb against the plump pinkness, and she parted her lips instantly. He focused there, so that she couldn't read his eyes.

"You are offering me—a guy who's had a raging hard-on for you all weekend—one night of mind-blowing sex, no strings?"

She took a deep breath. "Yes."

It hurt, playing it this way when he wanted so much more from her. He wouldn't think about it now—he wanted her enough to ignore the bigger picture—but yeah, he had high hopes she'd change her mind, that this was only the beginning.

"Hell yes. I'm in."

Her mouth was warm, wet, and willing, and his mind raced ahead to how she'd taste and feel in other places.

He was all in, all right. Whether he'd walk away without fighting for her was another question altogether.

———

Kalpani came awake at predawn in Jonah's arms with a smile. Despite little sleep, she felt amazing. Perfect, content, happy. She smoothed a hand along the lean muscles of his back and wished she could stay here until the noon checkout.

"I wish we could no-show," Jonah murmured as he nuzzled her neck and traced a finger under her breast. He meant the Sunday morning post-reception breakfast at the Sweetwater Inn.

"Me too. But I'm not too keen on being seen in my bridesmaid dress this morning, either."

Jonah's deft hands smoothed from her shoulder, along her back and butt, and, well…

She'd already discovered that sex with Jonah was epically good. His hands were magic, his mouth left her panting, his body was all hard male perfection, and her needs came first for him. But best of all were his green eyes. They held hers, binding them even deeper than their bodies could. She had never felt this connected during sex. He seemed to worship her, even cherish her—and that was a powerful, powerful thing.

Needless to say, the desire to experience it once more before sneaking away was too tempting.

An hour later, early morning light had crept into the room. They lay on their sides facing each other, and Jonah was threading her long hair through his fingers intently.

"What are you smiling about?" she asked.

"Your hair."

She already knew he liked it—wrapped in his fist, fanned out over his thighs, curled around her breasts…

He said, "It shines. In this light, with purples and reds." He tore his eyes from her hair to her face. "I've been working on a new piece of art, maybe a new line, but I'm not sure yet. And now I see that it's too black, too flat. It needs more color."

"I'm glad I could be of assistance."

His smile grew, as if he had a secret, but then he glanced at the ever-brightening sky.

She had the urge to put off their parting, and said, "It's cool with me if you keep coming to work upstairs."

He froze for a second then shook his head with a grin. "It was you who left me that food."

She smiled back. "You looked like you needed sustenance."

"Why didn't you boot my ass out?"

"I like your ass just as it is." She grinned and slid her knee along his thigh.

"Lucky me."

"You can come in the daytime. I cleared it with Lou. It shouldn't even be that loud now." If he came in the daytime, she might see him again after all.

"Thanks," he said. "I appreciate that. I am looking for space, but so far…" He made a face, and she understood that everything he'd seen had been crap.

They both looked at the window.

She said, "Hate to say, but…"

He nodded, his expression serious. "It's time."

They rose, cleaned up, and dressed, Jonah in jeans and a long-sleeved t-shirt that looked just as good as that tux; her in her dress and heels from the wedding. She had a coat downstairs in the front closet, at least. This early in the morning, winter frost would coat everything, and Jonah insisted she wear his fleece over her dress as well.

She looked at the gorgeous room—all bright colors and

gleaming wood with a Mexican pattered bench and gauzy drapes—and then at the tangled sheets. Her heart clenched. She wasn't fooling herself. Phenomenal sex wasn't all she'd miss. Jonah was an ideal combination between fun and sweet. Somehow, he managed to make things exciting and yet keep them low-key. Never sappy, yet always thoughtful and considerate. He was a good guy. Truly, a good guy.

He'd even offered to wait in True Springs with her until Monday, when the part for her car arrived from the auto repair. But she'd known that he was driving his mom back. And although surely Rita could have gotten another ride, Kalpani loved that Jonah was so attentive and close to Rita. She'd noticed yesterday that he kept one eye on Rita all day—gauging her well-being at what surely was a day of mixed emotions.

Kalpani had also declined Jonah's offer to stay because she'd said one night, and she'd meant one night.

Jonah tilted her chin up for a kiss. Soft, sweet, yet intimate—a kiss that promised so much more. So much that she wouldn't let herself have. She shut her eyes against the swift pang of hurt and breathed deeply of his warm, unique cinnamon scent.

"Ready?" he said.

She nodded and turned toward the door. But no—no, she wasn't ready to walk away from Jonah at all.

**14**

———————

It had been almost a week since the wedding and Jonah was starting to think he'd dreamed the amazing night with Kalpani. Monday he'd had other places he had to be, but Tuesday midday, he went to "work" upstairs at her salon. He didn't feel like he could show too early or stay all day. Lou seemed cool about the new arrangement, so Jonah kept the same schedule Wednesday and Thursday, arriving after lunch and staying until eight or nine at night. He kept hoping Kalpani might stop by after work.

Mornings he went to the gym or took a run. Once he'd played basketball with his brothers but had endured so many questions and ribbing about Kalpani that it was torturous. No problem if he'd had answers—but he didn't. She hadn't texted—even after he'd reached out on Monday afternoon.

*Hey, it's Jonah. Hope your car is good and you made it home no problem. Wish we were still holed up together at that inn. Back to reality is not that fun.*

He'd thought he'd hit the right note: somewhere

between *I'm not pressuring you* and *I can't stop thinking about you.* He'd thought he'd left her a lot of room to handle it however she wanted. She could have written back in any number of ways:

*Hey, I wish we were, too. How about a booty call?*

*Hey, I'm rethinking my rule. Want to have dinner?*

*Hey, car's fine, no trouble. Thanks for asking.*

But she hadn't even responded, which stung. There was no way she hadn't felt what he had. They'd connected on a far deeper level than just sex. He was sure of it.

Thursday evening, he realized he was being completely unproductive. He was moving the mouse, but his ear might as well have been pressed to the floorboard. Lou's subs had packed up a couple of hours ago. Jonah finally closed up his work and decided to head to The Wanderlust to eat. His mom would still be there, maybe Jake and Sadie, too, although he could never be sure of their schedule.

When Jonah entered, Rita was in the middle of showing some clients pictures of the wedding on her phone. Jonah chuckled. She probably hadn't stopped talking about it all week.

She waved to him and soon enough met him in the kitchen, where he chatted with Benny, their longtime alternate chef, and Sal, tonight's dishwasher. Jake and Sadie did indeed have the night off.

Rita began with her usual question: "Have you eaten?"

"I got him, Mrs. W," Sal said.

Rita had eaten already but joined him in a booth away from the other customers to visit.

"So," Rita said, "you and Kalpani were quite cozy at the wedding."

Luckily, he'd just taken a big bite of chicken parmesan.

"Are you going to ask her out?"

Jonah forced himself to swallow and wiped his mouth. "I don't know, Mom. She told me from the beginning she wasn't interested in dating."

"Why?"

He shrugged. "Don't know."

Kalpani hadn't offered a reason or explained at all. Other than the fact that she didn't believe in happy endings, he knew very little. Didn't she see what was right in front of them? Had she not attended the same wedding as the rest of them? Jeremy and Darcy definitely checked the happy-ending box.

"I saw—*everyone* saw—how she looked at you." Rita crossed her arms over her chest. "She might be saying one thing and wishing for another. And you're a catch."

Jonah rolled his eyes. "You are more than a little biased, Mom."

"Any girl would be lucky to have you, Jonah."

He appreciated the vote of confidence, and he'd certainly fielded plenty of interested females over the years. But by his age, Jake had gone so hard as a trader in New York that he owned a Manhattan loft and felt secure enough to walk away, and Jeremy had already opened his own music club and was making it work. Some women— maybe women as motivated as Kalpani—might consider Jonah a slacker. She'd alluded to as much, at first, anyway. He thought she'd gotten over it, but who knew.

He wasn't especially worried about marching to anyone else's timeline. So it had taken him a while to figure out the right path. So what? Money and security would follow talent, given enough hard work and enough time. That was what he was concentrating on.

"Ask her out anyway," Rita said. "Women like to know you're willing to fight for them."

Jonah saw a gleam in her eye. *Ho-whoa*—apparently, now that Jake and Jeremy were both married, her sights were set on him.

"Kalpani's not your average woman." Instinctively, he knew that pushing Kalpani would only send her running. His best bet still was to bump into her and hope he could finagle spending more time with her.

One thing was for certain, though. If she gave him half a chance—even the smallest opening—he'd be all over it.

## 15

W ithout even trying, Kalpani had found out Jonah's new schedule from her contractor. Now that she knew it, she couldn't get it out of her head.

She forced herself to stay away at first, but as she finished up with her last client Friday evening, she decided it was time. Maybe dropping off Jonah's fleece—instead of looking at it folded on the front seat of her car every day— would put last weekend behind her.

Kalpani grabbed a lint roller and tried to get hours' worth of hair bits off her black shirt, then pulled her long sweater, purse, and coat from her locker. She popped into the bathroom, used mouthwash, and reapplied lipstick— and pretended it wasn't because she might see Jonah.

By the time she reached Xanadu, the upstairs light to Jonah's little room was dark. The tension of anticipation released, and her shoulders dropped.

She shook her head. She'd said she didn't want any drama after the fact, and beyond one short text message, he'd honored that. He'd seemingly let her walk away. So, what the hell was her problem?

She clutched his fleece tight with one arm and stuck her key in the door as she turned the handle, but it suddenly swung open. She lost her balance, tumbling inside.

Strong hands grasped her upper arms and her body ended up flush against—

*Jonah.*

Her heart leapt, and a big smile erupted on her face.

Jonah grinned back, and his eyes twinkled. "You missed me after all."

Then his lips were on hers, and she forgot to breathe, let alone her pretense for coming tonight.

She slid her hands into his hair. He lifted her up, then set her down again further inside. He yanked out her keys and shoved the door shut. They never stopped kissing.

Her keys hit the floor with a clang, and he slid his hands over her back, along her waist, up her ribs. Then her breasts were in his hands and she could admit it—*Waheguru*—she'd missed him.

He feasted on her neck, and she moaned then slid her hands up under his flannel shirt. His skin was warm, his muscles were hard, and she remembered exactly how beautiful he was when undressed. She unbuttoned his shirt as fast as she could. He backed her against the wall, pushed one of her breasts up and out of her bra, and sucked her nipple through her shirt.

She gasped and rocked her pelvis against his thigh. Once, twice—he sucked hard—and she was riding him, already racing toward—

He grabbed her hips, stilling her. He kissed her, then

laid his forehead against hers. He was breathing as heavily as she was—*why* was he hitting the brakes?

"Have dinner with me."

She blinked.

"Don't get the wrong idea," he said. "I want you"—his eyes fastened on her lips, and she thought he might kiss her again—"more than ever. But I also want you to know that I like you, and not just this." His thigh pressed between her legs, emphasizing the point.

"Just making sure I have this right," she said. "You want to forgo sex." She slid her fingers ever so slowly down his chest and grabbed the waistband of his jeans, dipping her fingers inside. She was gratified to see his every muscle twitch under her touch. "To have dinner?"

"With you. Right now." Jonah's jaw clenched.

As badly as she wanted him, maybe it was just as well. Did she want to christen Xanadu with fast and furious sex right here in the entryway—the first place she'd soon see on a daily basis? Better, perhaps, to be reminded of hugs and kisses—although that didn't do justice to the passion they had just experienced.

He was looking at her so intently that she couldn't make herself say something flip.

"Okay."

Jonah smiled, although he still looked serious as all get out as he released her hips. He buttoned his shirt; she tucked herself back into her bra. He held her gaze, heat still emanating between them.

"Where to?" she asked.

He scooped up her keys. "Do you have a favorite? Indian, maybe?"

She shook her head. "It never compares to my mom's."

"Don't I know it. I haven't even bothered since you brought me those samosas."

They exited the building, and as soon as she put a foot to the cement stoop, she landed on something soft.

She bent and retrieved Jonah's fleece. "Look what I dropped on the way in. I wonder how that happened."

"It was quite a greeting." His eyes twinkled and he tossed it inside.

The bigger restaurants were jammed with Friday night crowds, so they decided on take out from Little Bangkok and returned to Xanadu to eat it.

Soon there would be benches and pillows in the front windows and a couple of chairs to match. Right now, there was Jonah's single chair upstairs or a metal ladder. The floor was dirty and dusty. Jonah laid the fleece down on the floor in front of the receptionist's desk and insisted she sit on it. He returned from upstairs with a big sheet of brown craft paper and spread the food out on it like a makeshift picnic, then he sat beside her.

"Your jeans," she said.

"They'll wash."

They leaned their backs against the reception desk and talked as they ate. Jonah asked about her family, how she knew she wanted to be a stylist, and about her plans for the salon. He talked some about Sohel, then said, "I want to show you something." Jonah went upstairs and returned with a sheaf of papers.

She looked at the first page and knew. "Sohel's will."

"Go to the end," Jonah said.

"He never signed it." Her heart lurched. "It was supposed to be yours, at least in Sohel's heart."

He nodded.

"That's… I'm so sorry."

"Don't be. I only wanted you to know why I was so thrown when you first showed up here. I'd made Sohel a promise to carry on for him. I thought I'd be doing that." Kalpani reached out and squeezed his hand. He squeezed back and smiled. "I think Sohel would be okay with the way things are turning out."

She leaned over and pressed a firm, lingering kiss to his lips. "Thank you for saying that."

They returned to their meal, and she asked if he'd heard from the honeymooning couple and how his art sales were these days. And he explained why he'd taken so many photos at the wedding: he hadn't yet given Jeremy and Darcy a gift, and he wanted to do a series of small pieces with their special people as a keepsake.

"I love that idea," she said. "Darcy will, too."

Everything new she learned about Jonah cemented what she'd already learned. He was a good guy: loyal, caring, and thoughtful. She smiled again—and then realized she smiled a lot in his presence.

They had kept the lights low, and with the front windows still taped over, it was like they were cocooned in their own little world. Just like last weekend, she found herself wishing it didn't have to end.

———

Per their usual Saturday morning routine, Kalpani and Darcy walked from their yoga class at Exhale to 21st Street Coffee and Tea. Darcy and Jeremy had taken only a short honeymoon because Jeremy didn't want to be away from the club too long while they were still instituting so many changes. In fact, they hadn't told their wedding guests, but they'd actually stayed in True Springs a few more days, renting a cottage on the outskirts of town and hiding out, just the two of them.

"We had groceries delivered ahead, then farm-fresh milk and eggs in the mornings so we could just stay in bed and—"

"Don't say any more." Kalpani held up a hand. "Now that you are married, I don't think I'm supposed to be privy to the nitty-gritty."

Darcy laughed. "Don't go all prude on me now. It was plain as day where you were headed last weekend."

"What do you mean?" Kalpani turned as if she were perusing the menu. In reality, she and Darcy knew the offerings here as well as they knew their own refrigerators.

"Tell me you didn't sleep with Jonah," Darcy said.

"Shh!" Kalpani bugged her eyes out at Darcy.

"Okay, fine," Darcy whispered. "But seriously." She watched Kalpani's face carefully, but Kalpani couldn't keep the corners of her mouth from turning up.

Darcy mouthed, *Oh my God.*

They ordered, and as soon as they had peeled out of their winter coats and sat, Darcy said. "Since he's now my brother-in-law, I don't want details." She squished her eyes shut as if blocking out the thought. "But I need—you know—details."

Kalpani shook her head.

"Fine. Just…I know how you are. One date, one night, whatever, and you prefer to move on. But you and Jonah actually seemed really in sync."

Kalpani leaned back in her chair with a big rush of breath. "We were. We are. I don't know."

Darcy raised an eyebrow over her coffee cup.

"Your wedding festivities were like some fairytale date. And then that night? Let me just say *wow*."

Darcy buried her face in her hands but recovered quickly.

"I hadn't seen him again until last night, when I bumped into him at the salon."

"What's he doing at Xanadu?"

"Working. Remember his equipment is upstairs in storage? Except he's actually using the computers and printers. At first, it was on the sly at night, but I gave him the green light so… Anyway, last night. He was leaving as I was arriving to check on things, and…"

"Oh my God," Darcy said, eyes wide. "At the salon?"

"No! We grabbed dinner. Very casual." Darcy definitely didn't need to know about the hot and heavy start to the evening.

Darcy shook her head. "And?"

"And it was nice. Perfect, really."

Darcy clapped her hands.

"No," Kalpani said. "Don't do that."

"Why? It's exciting."

"Uh-uh, it's not good."

"Why not?" Darcy looked truly baffled.

"Because I don't want to like him. I don't want a man. I don't want to be tied down."

Darcy said, "From what? Speed dating every weekend? Jumping out of planes? Jetting off to Club Med?" Kalpani cocked her head to the side, and Darcy made a face back. "You pretty much work all the time, do yoga a few times a week, and visit your family."

Darcy wasn't wrong. But she was missing the point. "I've told you before. I'm never going to marry."

Darcy stared at her. Finally, she said, "I'm not sure why spending time with someone you enjoy automatically equates to him handing you a ring made of cement blocks and chains."

"It always ends up there. Everyone wants that. I really like Jonah—too much. It feels extra wrong to lead him on, when I know I'll break it off in the end."

Neither of them had begun to eat yet, so Darcy cut her quiche and transferred half to Kalpani's plate, then did the opposite with Kalpani's scone. Kalpani's appetite had fled suddenly, but Darcy broke off a corner of the scone and nibbled.

"So," she said, "you don't want to bother because you assume this will go all the way, and he'll undoubtedly want to get married someday?"

Kalpani rubbed her eyes. It sounded so stupid when it was put like that. But she had her reasons.

"You know," Darcy said, "it is possible that he dumps your conceited ass *before* you have a chance to crush him." She winked and popped a bite of scone into her mouth.

Kalpani laughed. Darcy hardly ever swore, but when she did, it was usually with great effect.

"Listen, I'm hardly any expert on any of this." Darcy leaned forward. "But did you ever consider that just maybe it's okay to let something run its course? And okay to *not* make it a big deal? If you like Jonah and he makes you feel good, hang out with him." She shrugged. "If you stop liking him, break it off." Another shrug. "It doesn't have to fit into one of your goals."

"You make it sound so easy." A surge of excitement or

maybe hope bumped around inside of Kalpani. She squeezed her knees together under the table.

"Exactly my point. Maybe this could just be easy."

Kalpani had been fighting the desire to see Jonah since the wedding, but what Darcy said made a lot of sense. Was Kalpani grasping for an excuse to keep seeing Jonah? Or had Darcy just given Kalpani some much-needed perspective?

**16**

———

J onah wasn't sure what had changed, but Kalpani had joined him at Xanadu the last three evenings. On Monday, she'd texted out of the blue to see if he'd be there. He was—and wasn't about to leave if she was on her way. When she arrived, they went down the block to Pho Van for a casual dinner. When they'd later locked up Xanadu, he'd given her a very thorough goodnight kiss. It'd about killed him to stop there, but he was wary of pushing her too far, too fast.

They planned to meet Tuesday, then Wednesday…and by Thursday, Jonah realized that seeing Kalpani each evening had become an expectation rather than a hope.

That evening, she pounded up the stairs to his cramped work area before he even had a chance to wrap up.

"I have to talk to you." She wore yoga pants and her puffy coat and had her hair in a sloppy bun on top of her head. Somehow, she looked both hot and adorable—and very serious.

"Okay." Jonah felt a wash of worry.

"I saw that new piece of art you put up at that place next to the winery. The really big one? It has a sold tag already?" Her words rushed out and her eyes were bright.

He smiled. Of course, he knew exactly which one she'd meant: a large piece emphasizing a forceful black swirl and bursts of black flowers enhanced with red and purples on a white background. He'd added some sparkling silver after printing to give it a little more life. This one represented the fierce power and beauty of a strong woman—not that anyone would know that but him. "You like?"

"I love it. It's stunning."

"Excellent." Jonah grinned.

"I want to buy it."

"You can't."

She raised her chin. "I'll pay double."

"You can't." Jonah laughed. She really did love it—this was perfect.

Kalpani pressed her lips together then grabbed his arm and tugged him to the stairs. "Come with me."

She dragged him all the way to the front of Xanadu and turned him to face the reception desk.

"Look. Can't you picture it right here? For every person who walks in the door to see?" She looked hard at him.

He tilted his head, pretending to consider it.

Kalpani tried again. "Can't you just print out another one?"

Jonah shook his head. "It's one of a kind. The owner isn't going to want it duplicated."

Kalpani crossed her arms over her chest. "I want the

name of the owner, then. I'll have to convince them to sell it to me."

"That won't be a problem." He wrapped an arm around her and tried to kiss her, but she pushed against his chest.

"Why?"

"Because the owner is you."

"What are you talking about?"

"I created it for you, Kalpani Desai, owner of Xanadu. For that very spot." He pointed to the wall she'd made him look at. "I was worried you might not like it, though."

She looked at the ceiling, muttering, *"Durga,* a little help, please." Then, with a calming breath, she looked at Jonah. "Why in the world is it in that window, then? With a sold tag, no less?"

"It's a departure for me, so I wanted to see if people responded. You know, to see if I should do a line in a similar vein," Jonah said. "The sold tag is because I didn't want to risk them selling it accidentally."

A smile grew on Kalpani's lips and she pressed her hands together at her heart. "It's really mine?"

"Now will you kiss me?"

She rose on tiptoes and wrapped her arms around his neck. He could feel her smile in the kiss.

"Wait." She pulled back. "We need to finish this discussion. What do I owe you?"

"Nothing," he said.

"Come on. You could get— Well, I don't know what, but a lot of money for it."

"It was always meant for you, as a gift for your grand opening."

"Jonah…"

"If it makes you feel better, consider the fact that you

saved me loads of rent by allowing me to continue to work upstairs," he said. "But I didn't do it to make us even. I did it because I wanted to. You inspired that piece of art. It's been yours from the beginning."

He reached out and undid her topknot, then pulled the strands through his fingers. "But I knew I was missing something and couldn't finish it until I got it just right."

"The colors in my hair?"

He smiled, thinking back to lying naked and sated with Kalpani in True Springs. "Yes."

Kalpani's eyes glistened. "Thank you." She wrapped her arms around him, and he hugged her back. "How long do you need it to stay in the window?"

"Until you are ready to hang it," he said. "So sometime after the place is painted and before opening day."

She nodded, then her hands flew to her mouth. "Oh, no. I have to change my sign. Out front."

"You ordered one? You said you couldn't decide."

"I couldn't, but I was afraid of it not being ready in time. I placed the order today," she said. "I went with the simple san serif font, figuring it'd be safer in the long run. But the other one, the one with some flair—the one I really liked—would be a much better match for your art."

"Creating more of a theme."

She nodded. "A brand. I'm sure they haven't started the sign yet. I'll call them." She swatted him. "When were you going to tell me?"

"Tonight." He chuckled. "I was going to talk you into dinner out tonight and swing you by there on the way. But I'm glad you saw it first. Teasing you was way more fun."

"You, Jonah Walker, will pay for that."

"Gladly," he said, and hoped he'd be anteing up some of those dues very, very soon.

———

Kalpani had never invited a man to her place, but she invited Jonah. The man had created a spot-on, gorgeous work of art just for her. The least she could do was feed him a good meal of her mother's *bhartha* and *channa*. Kalpani could make the dishes, of course, but she couldn't quite attain the perfection her mother managed so easily.

As it turned out, they didn't eat first. Both of them were primed to touch after he'd halted their romp last weekend and then they'd spent so much time together all week. The sex was—in short—astounding. The food hadn't suffered for waiting, either.

Like every other time she spent with Jonah, Kalpani didn't want it to be over. The little town of True Spring's silly legend crossed her mind. She and Jonah had both drunk the water, but— No. She shook her head. That was just ridiculousness. What did hold some weight, however, was Darcy's reasonable take on dating. Kalpani considered this, then threw the last of her reservations out the window, and invited Jonah to stay the night.

"I'll let my mom know," Jonah said.

Kalpani looked at the clock. They'd just finished the dishes, but it was eleven p.m. "Won't she be sleeping?" She hated for Rita to think badly of her. Her own parents would be truly horrified. She often pushed them to be more American and more twenty-first century about so many things—not that they listened, but even she felt uncomfortable about this.

"If she wakes in the night, realizes I'm not there, and starts to worry? I don't want to do that to her," Jonah said.

"Are you going to tell her where you're staying?"

He laughed. "She's been pushing me to ask you out since the wedding, and she knows we've spent time together this week. She'd have a fit if I led her to believe I was anywhere else."

"Maybe you should just go home."

Jonah laughed. "You don't get to take back that invite." He pulled her to him, and his hard length pressed into her belly. She looked up at him, shaking her head, but he bent and kissed her like there was no tomorrow.

When she'd nearly forgotten about the necessary phone call, he said, "It'll be fine, promise."

Rita answered his call right away. He told her, "I'm going to stay at Kalpani's."

He shook his head at something Rita said, then mouthed, *Condoms*, at Kalpani.

Horrified, she pressed her hands to her eyes.

Sleeping curled into Jonah all night was worth it, and soon that became part of their new routine as well.

Darcy had been right—when Kalpani stopped projecting, it felt easy. It felt right.

A couple of weeks went by in this manner. They both had work and obligations, but they saw each other most evenings and spent most nights together at her place. Neither had to be up especially early, and mornings became a special time together, too—sometimes lazily exploring each other in bed, sometimes making breakfast or grabbing a quick bite together before a morning work-out. He ran or played ball with his brothers, and she went to yoga or sometimes took a long walk along one of the river paths.

Xanadu was due to open next week, but it became clear that the contractor was going to be hard-pressed to finish every detail in time. She walked around Xanadu creating a list. He'd begun painting, but also needed to install knobs on the cabinetry and the hardware in the bathrooms, the kick plates in front of every chair, and the shelving in the cabinets and storeroom. Plus, they had to have final inspections, get the security system installed—

*Oh, Durga*—the list went on and on and was overwhelming.

She threw the pen and pad on the counter.

"What's wrong?" Jonah massaged her shoulders, and she heaved out a breath.

It was Thursday, and Xanadu's grand opening was next Wednesday, March eighteenth—less than a week for absolutely everything to be completed, stocked, and cleaned. Kalpani tried not to freak out.

"There's simply not enough time to get it all done. There's not much choice," she said. "The upstairs painting will have to wait. Still, I'm afraid it will be weeks before Lou can come back. He's already got most of his guys on another project."

"You and I could paint up there," Jonah said. "Maybe he could knock something off your grand total."

She opened her mouth, then closed it again, considering. "You'd do that?"

"Of course."

Kalpani had already given notice at her other salon and allowed herself a week off between to make sure she was organized, ready, and could deal with any last-minute problems. So, she had the time, and this certainly qualified.

"That could work. I want those upstairs rooms usable. And if you and I were both painting, it would go pretty fast."

As it turned out, they worked as well together on a painting project as they did in bed.

On Sunday, when they were punchy and starving, but nearly finished—only the second coat with rollers to finish in the last room—Kalpani looked up at Jonah and laughed.

"You have paint in your hair again." He was so flipping sexy in a fitted t-shirt and paint-speckled sweatpants that sat low on his hips.

He did another few strokes, then set his roller in the pan and climbed off the ladder. "That's nothing," he said. "You have it under your shirt."

"What? Where?"

He nodded and spun her around, lifting up her t-shirt in the back. "When you were bent over, I could see it." He circled it with one warm fingertip.

"Mmm, and here I thought you were looking at my butt."

"Oh, I was." He gave her tush a squeeze. "All that wiggling has been drawing my eye."

She laughed, and he stepped in to kiss her. She looped her arms around his neck.

"Put that roller down first."

She laughed. "Oops."

She returned her roller to her pan, and then he advanced on her.

"I take it you need a break."

"There's a distraction calling me."

She smiled and stepped into him. "I suppose drop cloths could serve a dual purpose."

"Exactly what I was thinking."

And "oops" was right. When she pulled his t-shirt off him and ran her hands up his muscled back to his shoulders, she realized she'd dripped so much mauve paint on him that it'd soaked right through to his skin.

"We have to be fast," she said. "The paint..." But Jonah was already kissing her, with his big hands roaming over her skin.

"Not a problem," he murmured into her neck. "There's never a time I don't already want you."

**17**

---

J onah brought a nice bottle of wine to Kalpani's, along with some takeout Italian.

"To Xanadu's grand opening," Jonah said, raising his wine glass to Kalpani's in the privacy of her apartment. "May your salon be everything you dreamed."

"Cheers." Kalpani wore a huge smile, although Jonah knew she'd been running on adrenaline and nerves.

Their dinner conversation centered entirely on Xanadu, as it should on this momentous night. Everything had come together. The painting was done, the art he'd made for her was hung and looked right at home, and the sign she'd ordered had been mounted outside. The cushions for the built-in seating in the front window were in place, the stock of fancy hair products sat on the shelves ready for purchase, and magazines were even fanned out on the low tables.

Jonah had met a few of her stylists and assistants, because they'd been in Monday and Tuesday for training and bonding. Between her and the stylists, Xanadu had quite a few clients scheduled already. Kalpani's payment system worked—he'd bought some seriously stiff hair gel to prove it. She'd ordered balloons for outside and savory nibbles and sweets to make the grand opening special, and she and her staff would toast with champagne right before opening the doors. She even had a visit from a local reporter scheduled.

God forbid the reporter wanted a full tour, though. "I still wish I'd gotten out of your space upstairs on time," Jonah said. They were finished eating, and he corked the wine.

"I told you, it's fine," Kalpani said. "I haven't found the right massage therapist yet anyway." She'd graciously offered for him to stay another couple of months.

She noticed his discomfort and came around the little dining table in her apartment to sit on his lap. "I'm sure if I hadn't kept you so busy painting and other things"—she winked—"you'd have had more time to look for studio space."

"Those other things definitely took priority." He'd put off any timeline if it meant more time with Kalpani, in or out of bed. Jonah settled her across his thighs right where he wanted her. She was so small that she weighed next to nothing, but somehow they fit together perfectly.

She wriggled and kissed him. He slid his hand up her shirt, gratified when her nipples perked into his fingers. But he didn't let it go too far. It was important for her to turn in early tonight, so he smoothed her shirt back down and leaned his forehead against hers.

"I'm going," he said. She didn't know it, but he also had his own agenda to keep tonight.

They made quick work of the dishes, and he kissed her

thoroughly once more to make it last. He'd make himself scarce tomorrow, not even slipping up the back stairs to work. He wanted her to just be able to do her thing.

"I don't know how I'm going to sleep," she said. "I just know I forgot something or—"

"Shh. It's going to be great."

Jonah left, smiling to himself. He knew at least one thing Kalpani had forgotten: business cards. Luckily, he'd realized it with time to create some on the sly. He'd matched the wording on her sign, combined it with a bit from the art he'd created, and added Xanadu's information and her name with the word *owner*. He figured if she liked them, he could do them for each stylist to keep at their station. If she didn't, she could just tell him what she wanted, and he'd go at it again.

He drove to the Strip District and was relieved that he could still park behind the shop. Tonight was Saint Patty's Day, and the Strip was jammed with drunk partygoers who'd been at it since happy hour. Jonah got a kick out of the revelry, but this year, he was perfectly happy not to be participating.

The weeks since Jeremy's wedding had been so great. He'd been surprised when the one-night-only mandate Kalpani had set out had naturally evolved into actually being exclusive. They hadn't talked that through, but that was the case. Maybe because it had happened so naturally, maybe because he hadn't pushed her, maybe because he'd let her come to him... Who knew? Maybe it was just meant to be.

He'd recently done a lot of thinking about what he wanted from a relationship. And he wanted what his parents had had, and what both Jake and Jeremy appeared to have found. Love and passion, of course, but also a true partnership—enhanced by mutual respect, admiration, and commitment.

He and Kalpani were on that path. He was sure of it. He'd never felt as drawn to a person, and the more time they spent together and the better he got to know her, the more he felt they had something real and solid.

Jonah looked at the shop. All vestiges of Sohel's Print & Ship were gone. He wasn't bitter, or even wistful. He was glad Kalpani was the new owner, and that he'd been a part of it. Exiting the car, he grabbed the brown gift bag for Kalpani. In addition to the box of business cards, he'd purchased a cool, hand-crafted card holder from a local artisan.

He put his key in the lock, turned it and the handle, and pushed open the door. A beeping and flashing came from the wall near his left shoulder.

"Oh, shit." Kalpani hadn't yet gotten a new locksmith out, but she had just had the new alarm system installed—and he'd forgotten all about it. She hadn't given him the code and—

He pushed the door shut behind him, flipped on the light, pushed a button—

*No, no, no.* He had no idea how to turn it off.

The phone rang and he darted to answer it, but the service representative wanted the owner's information and code word. She asked numerous questions that he couldn't answer.

"Sir, please stay where you are."

An alarm blasted out of nowhere, and Jonah jumped and covered his other ear with his hand. Oh, Christ, they were going to send the cops, he just knew it.

"Kalpani Desai is the owner. I'm her boyfriend." He spoke fast, panic surging through his body. He flipped on another light, not wanting to be caught here in the dark. "I just came to drop something off, I swear. Completely forgot to ask her for the code. The alarm is brand new."

He was still trying to talk his way out of this when he heard sirens growing louder. Flashing lights appeared both in front of and behind the salon in moments.

He swore. That was fast, but cruisers and patrol officers were already out in force down here for all the drunk leprechauns.

"I'm going to open the doors," Jonah told the woman on the phone. He didn't even know if she was speaking with the police, but he wasn't taking any chances. He set the receiver down, walked slowly to unlock the front door, and used the kick stop to prop it open. He saw two cops jump out of their cars.

With leaden steps, he crossed to the back door and opened it as well. He couldn't see the cops out back—too dark, too strobe-light-ish.

Jonah returned to stand in the middle of the space— purposely positioning himself where he was visible from both directions.

With a chirp, the sirens quieted, and in seconds, officers had converged at both ends of the room. Two approached slowly—obviously cautious and yet acting casual—except that one had a hand hovering near his holster.

*Ho-whoa,* his mother would kill him if he got himself shot. Or even taken down to the station.

Jonah raised his arms and was surprised to realize he still held the bag with Kalpani's gifts.

He launched into an explanation, and this time, luckily one of the cops recognized his name.

"Chuck Walker's son?"

"Yeah."

"Sorry about your dad. I eat at The Wanderlust often. Your mom seems to be holding up."

"She's doing okay. Thanks."

"Didn't you used to work here?"

By this time, the officers had all relaxed—thank God—and one called in to have the alarm reset, so, blessedly, the blaring stopped.

Jonah explained that yes, he'd worked at the Print & Ship for years, that yes, Sohel had been a fixture in this neighborhood forever, and that now he and the new owner were dating.

One of the other officers still wrote him out a ticket. He ripped it off, and Jonah accepted it with his free hand.

He gulped. "What's the charge?"

At that moment, Kalpani flew in the door wild-eyed with her hair half falling out of a bun. He'd only left her maybe thirty minutes ago or so. She'd washed her makeup off and now wore sleep pants, a tank, and a long sweater she must have pulled on as she ran out the door.

*Double shit.* Of course the alarm agency would have called the owner. Jonah's heart sank. Any hope of salvaging his surprise fled—even worse, Kalpani looked both upset and furious.

"What the hell is going on?" she said.

"Well, miss, your boyfriend here—"

She narrowed her eyes and glared.

"He is your boyfriend, isn't he?"

Her nostrils flared and her fists clenched. For a second,

Jonah feared she'd say no—they'd never discussed termi-
nology—but she gave a tight nod.

He let out a breath. Okay, at least he wasn't going to
end up in jail.

"I forgot about the security system," he said. "But I'm
sure to them it looked like…" He was at a loss. "What is
the charge?" He held up the ticket in question, praying it
didn't carry any criminal charges or hefty fines.

The officer who'd written out the ticket said, "Simple
trespass."

Kalpani lunged forward and grabbed it.

Jonah felt a strong zap of electricity run up his arm and
jerked back.

She jumped, too.

The ticket tore down the middle.

"Ow! What'd you do that for?" she asked.

"I didn't." Jonah crushed the remaining paper in his
fist. Yeah, the zap was weird, but she was spoiling for a
fight he wanted no part of.

She threw her hands up. "I told you weeks ago to start
coming during the day. And now—the night before
opening you are going to sneak in to work? I thought we
were past the antics."

"I wasn't sneaking in." Jonah's jaw clenched and his
whole body was strung tauter than his canvases. Their first
big fight and they had an audience of police officers—one
of whom knew his whole family? Friggin' excellent.

"It sure looks like it from here." Now her hands were
on her hips.

"There weren't any antics."

"Oh, really?"

One of the officers cleared his throat. Another said, "I think we're done here. Miss? You're okay?"

"Yes," she said, although it was uttered through gritted teeth.

"Okay, then, we'll leave you to it."

The officer who knew his parents gave Jonah a nod, and he managed one back.

"It's just a warning. Good luck," said the officer who wrote the ticket in a low voice as he passed Jonah. Great—even the police were wary of solo kitty's claws.

They left as they came, shutting the doors behind them.

Their exit gave Jonah just enough time to think, instead of reacting defensively. But his anger was only ramping up. Kalpani's accusation hit him hard.

Kalpani was breathing heavily. "What the hell, Jonah?"

"I could ask you the same thing," he said.

"What does that mean?"

"You walked in here and immediately assumed I was up to no good. That I was trying to pull something over on you."

"Because you are. You said you were going home to your mom's tonight. You never once mentioned coming down here. And we discussed that you'd come during the day when you needed to work—just not on opening day."

He shook his head. Anger now competed with frustration, disappointment, dismay—all warring for top spot.

"No matter how far we come, it's clear you'll never really let me in. I thought it was all in my head, but you still think of me as some freeloader, don't you?"

She opened her mouth to protest, but he threw the crumpled ticket to the floor and held up his hand. "You'll never trust me, never believe that I'm not trying to take something from you or take advantage of you."

"I just told you, you can have free access upstairs," she said, the words clipped. "You have at least a couple of months before I'll want to renovate that space."

"That's not what I'm talking about and you know it." Jonah fought to remain in place—to get out his thoughts, to tell her what he'd realized before he got the hell out of here. "You've been waiting for a chance to prove I can't be trusted. Nothing to do with me. I've proven myself to you over and over. You just can't see it. I don't know who wronged you, but I'm not going to pay their price."

Kalpani stood stock-still and stared at him.

He couldn't remotely gauge her thoughts. He'd been debating signing a studio lease on the outskirts of the Strip anyway. It wasn't perfect, and it was more than he wanted to pay, but it was immediately available. This—this debacle—sealed the deal.

"I'll move all my stuff out this Sunday and Monday when Xanadu's closed. I'm out. You didn't want a relationship from the beginning. So, congratulations. You don't have one. You're free of me."

Kalpani winced and blinked, but she didn't speak.

Jonah spun to go, and the bag he held bumped his hip.

He tossed it on the receptionist's counter with too much force. It slid and knocked the cordless phone he'd left off the hook to the floor with a bang.

"Happy opening," he said. Then Jonah stalked out the back door and left without looking back.

**18**

Kalpani watched Jonah leave, the door banging shut behind him. She stood rooted, eyes fixed on that door—still reeling from the turn of events.

She didn't know how many minutes had passed, but she snapped out of it when some drunken idiot bumped into the front window hard enough to make her jump. She was standing in a fishbowl—all the Strip District St. Patty's Day crowds able to see right in. She hadn't ordered window coverings—generally it was good advertising for people to be able to see into a salon. But right now, she only felt raw and exposed.

She rubbed her hands over her arms, then forced herself to move and lock the front door. When she turned back to the room, she eyeballed the bag Jonah had thrown on the counter but didn't reach for it. Instead, she picked up the crumpled paper—the other half of the ticket she still held. She shook her head and threw both in the trash behind the desk. She retrieved the phone that had fallen to the floor, checked to make sure it worked, and replaced it on the receiver.

Kalpani flipped off the lights and moved to the back of the store, locking that door as well. She checked that the alarm had been reset—and a tiny noise of upset escaped her. She covered her mouth with one hand and pulled her sweater across her front to ward off the chill. March in Pittsburgh wasn't that cold—all her discomfort stemmed from inside.

When she'd walked in—yes, dammit, she'd assumed the worst.

Not consciously. It was like this terrible fear had risen like floodwater and invaded her whole body. Like she had suddenly realized that she'd inadvertently given away the keys to the castle. The castle being, of course, her salon, her dream, her independence—right along with her foolish heart.

It had sent her into a complete panic. All she could think of was Meenu: on her wedding day, glowing with happiness, thinking she'd married—an American, no less—for love and a modern life. The look of shock and disbelief she'd worn the first time her husband had beaten her—making excuses for him while Kalpani's father had wrapped her ribs. The empty shell she'd become since: lifeless eyes, wooden movements, rote words—a woman always on edge and in control of nothing, a woman who owned nothing, not even her own voice.

Logically, Kalpani knew it wasn't the same. She wasn't Meenu. But they'd both been snowed. Like Meenu, Kalpani had never suspected a beast lived within her friend's husband. She hadn't entirely trusted her own judgment ever since.

And after a scary call from the alarm company about a possible break-in at her new salon, a frantic drive to Xanadu in the dark, the flashing lights of the police vehicles nearly giving her vertigo, and uniformed officers blocking the doorways, then Jonah standing there chatting like it was any other day?

Well, she certainly hadn't been thinking logically. Fear manifested in anger, and as always, she was adept at cutting words and a biting tone—a means of defense and protection both.

Kalpani smoothed one hand over the other, then, still chilled, she tucked her fingers under her armpits.

What in the hell had he been doing here?

He'd never answered the question, and that brown bag beckoned her. It felt dangerously stupid to ignore it, like a ticking time bomb resonating inside her head.

She knew without a doubt that opening it would make her feel even worse. She forced herself to go get it and brought it toward the back of the shop, where the walls of the hallway were closer, as if less space, perhaps, could contain an explosion.

She took a shaky breath and pulled apart the handles to peer inside. Tissue paper—stuffed down deep at the bottom. She grabbed the banister and sat heavily on the back steps, pressing the back of her hand to her mouth to stop her sob.

Jonah had tried to leave her a gift. Some sort of surprise for her opening day. It didn't even matter what was under that tissue paper. She'd thrown his thoughtful gesture in his face in the worst way, framed his actions in the worst light.

She sobbed, then swallowed it. With a shaking hand, she reached in to pull out the tissue.

She unwrapped a business card holder first. *Oh, no.*

With a wobbling lip and tears spilling from her eyes, she then opened a small cardboard box. Her very own Xanadu business cards—designed by Jonah, including a bit of the art he'd also gifted her with.

She'd been wrong. It did matter what was in the bag.

Grief won, and Kalpani broke down and sobbed something fierce.

Here was a man who actively tried to please her, who thought ahead about her needs, who went out of his way for her, who'd done nothing but support her throughout the construction of her salon…

She hadn't even given him the benefit of her trust.

Kalpani curled into a ball on those hard wooden steps and cried until she couldn't breathe, because she was sure she never could.

## 19

Xanadu's grand opening week should have felt celebratory, exciting, gratifying. Instead, the event was weighted with regret and even grief. Kalpani missed Jonah. She didn't know what to do or say about it and tried to convince herself it was just as well. She'd never intended to have a long-term relationship, hadn't meant for a casual thing to become so involved. She was the woman who was going to escape the bad parts of her culture, the dangerous parts of being a woman in a relationship. She had always meant to conquer the world alone and turn it upside down—or right side up.

But every time she handed out a business card or straightened the artistic little holder on the desk, underneath her business-owner smile—she hurt. Way down deep inside, she ached terribly. Because she missed him, because she'd wronged him, because life felt empty without him.

On Saturday, she pasted on an even bigger smile. Free from their own jobs, her parents came to see the salon.

"For you and your staff," Chetana said, handing her a heavy bag of foil wrapped packets. "Samosas and *chaat*."

"Thank you, *Mummyji*, you shouldn't have." Her mother had started cooking a day early and must have risen extremely early. Kalpani's eyes prickled.

She took time to give them a tour and smiled as they remarked on the oddest things. Her father had peered closely at the metal kick plates, going so far as to lean over a client's legs and touch one. She'd scolded him and mouthed, *So sorry*, to the client. Her mother had peeked into every closed cupboard she'd passed. "Where is the food?" she'd asked.

"It's a salon, not a restaurant." Kalpani fought to keep the irritation out of her voice. Jonah had never met her parents, but with his easy manner, he would have handled them so much better than she did.

They hadn't taken off their coats and soon gathered near the front door to say goodbyes.

"Well, Harvard would have been a surer bet," Chetana said, "but it's *beautiful*." She drew the adjective out with extra syllables and two hard Es, and Kalpani smiled.

She knew from their discussions over the last couple of months that her father, too, was still very concerned about the loan from Darcy and the risk she was taking in owning her own business. Today, she saw pride in his eyes as well. She wanted to cry, and silently cursed the emotional mess she'd become.

Shortly afterward, her phone buzzed in her apron, and her heart nearly burst out of her chest—*Jonah*—before it shriveled. The text read: *Moving out tomorrow. Disable alarm or send code.*

She moved sluggishly through the rest of the day. Her

thoughts were as thick with distress as the high-end finishing clay she often used on her male clients' hair.

Sunday morning, far earlier than usual due to her parents going to an afternoon event, she went to help her mom with the cooking. Just as well, since being alone with her thoughts right now was downright depressing.

Now that they'd seen Xanadu with their own eyes, they had a million questions about her first few days of operation. Kalpani told them stories—one of the sinks had leaked, one of the new assistants had called in sick, a client's scalp had had an allergic reaction, and more.

Honestly, overall opening week had gone well. Problems like that were part and parcel of owning a business, especially a brand-new one.

She should be elated, but she couldn't stop thinking about Jonah. She should have called him to apologize and to thank him for her business cards. But she had put it off. Absurdly, she felt like calling and having that last conversation would be somehow severing ties entirely. That—and what could she say? *You are totally right? I tried to warn you that I didn't want long term? I'm sorry?*

Yes, she was sorry. So dang sorry, but it didn't change anything, did it?

When her father picked up the crossword puzzle, her mom shooed her toward the kitchen. "Come," Chetana said. "There is much to do."

One step into the tight space, and Kalpani halted. Chetana had taped Xanadu's business card to the refrigerator. That little rectangle of cardstock sank her spirits even lower. It represented all that was beautiful about Jonah, and all that was withered in her.

Her mom shoved her forward and pointed to a cutting

board. Kalpani got to work cutting onions. She told herself that was what caused her eyes to tear.

"Not so hard, *beti*," Chetana said. "Don't force out the juice."

"Sorry," Kalpani said, but her voice cracked.

Her mother turned to her. "What is the matter?"

Kalpani sniffed. "Onions."

Her mother put her hands on her hips. "You think your *maan* is stupid?"

Indian mothers were not generally the type to coddle you if you were upset. They were more likely to swat you with a wooden spoon, order you to get your act together, and throw you out of their kitchen. But despite some skirmishes over cultural norms and generational differences, Kalpani had a decent relationship with hers.

"No, *Mummyji*, but I am stupid." That fact that she desperately needed someone to talk to made her admit things she normally wouldn't. "I think I might have accidentally fallen for someone."

Her mother's eyes narrowed, but her expression perked up—she was clearly torn between protecting her daughter and seeing her finally show interest in dating.

"Don't get excited." Kalpani heaved a sigh and began to tell her mother about Jonah.

Chetana interrupted often with questions. *How did you meet him? Why didn't you tell me? So, he is the youngest son and your friend Darcy married the middle son?* And more—though, thankfully, she didn't ask if they'd been sleeping together.

At one point, Chetana waved at the cutting board, requesting the onions and from then on, they worked as Kalpani spilled.

Finally, when they'd covered the trespassing incident, her mom stopped and put her hands to her mouth. "The police?"

Kalpani nodded. "Unfortunately, yes."

Her mother was horrified to learn she hadn't spoken to Jonah since, hadn't even apologized.

"Oh, *beti*, that is very bad. That is not the way you were raised."

"I know. It just feels loaded."

"Why?"

"Because I feel terrible. Jonah doesn't deserve that kind of treatment. He's a good guy. A really good guy. And I really, really like him."

"I don't understand what is the trouble."

A knock sounded from the living room, and Kalpani heard her father rise and go to the door. She heard a women's voice and a child's. As always, she tensed, her shoulders creeping toward her ears, but she purposely pushed away thoughts of injuries and past patients. She and her mother continued talking, ignoring her father's conversation to allow his patient some privacy.

Kalpani tried to explain to her mother how she felt about dating, about marriage, about—above all— remaining completely independent. But it sounded as nonsensical now as it did when she'd tried to explain it to Darcy, and she ended lamely, "I promised myself I would never, ever be dependent on anyone."

Her mother, however, understood. She had listened to the messages between Kalpani's words for years and years. She knew her daughter's fears almost as well as she knew her own.

"Why are you so worried about this? You broke the

mold every day since you were born. Look what you have accomplished already at such a young age. Should you decide to marry"—Chetana shot her eyes heavenward—"you will not be one who will fall into patterns of culture or traditional relationships. You will never be pushed by someone else's current."

She handed Kalpani a cup of chai tea and waved her to the small table tucked into a corner of the kitchen. She grabbed some sugar packets from a drawer overflowing with freebie condiments, then joined Kalpani there with her own teacup.

"Just because you made a decision when you were a young girl does not mean it is the right one for you. And if you choose to have a relationship, you can make it whatever you need. It does not need to model my marriage. I know what you think of that." She gave Kalpani a particularly hard look.

Kalpani winced at the set-down. Many times, she had pushed her mother to stand up for herself, to make her father help—at least a little bit—with the chores. Chetana was letting her know she didn't appreciate the disrespect and wouldn't forget it.

"But all the compromising," Kalpani said. "I don't want to ever have to go to someone for permission or approval or money or anything."

"Ah, but that person will also be compromising his own things for yours, too." Chetana set her spoon down, having added way more sugar than was healthy, and slurped loudly. She eyed Kalpani over the rim. "Walking through life with the right support at your side is not a bad thing or something to fight against. There is enough in the world to battle. Walking with someone at your side is to be embraced. The power of two is not a gift to be overlooked lightly."

Kalpani stirred her own tea, swirling it like the thoughts in her head. Darcy and Jeremy's wedding had really made her think. They were so in love it was ridiculous, but they also seemed to be respectful and supportive of each other. Jake and Sadie appeared to be much the same. Kalpani and Jonah had fallen into exclusivity, but he had never once hampered her. In truth, he'd been supporting her through what had proved to be a challenging time. Had all these Walker boys learned how to be great men from their parents? Surely, they didn't have a lock on the excellent husband role. There had to be others.

Had Kalpani just not been exposed to very many of those kinds of marriages—really balanced ones? The kind she might actually consider? It was true, of course, that most of the married people she knew well were of her own culture, and also true that most of those were from an older generation.

It was also quite possible that because she hadn't been open to the idea of an equal partnership, she had never looked with clear eyes. Certainly, Meena's situation had caused her to put additional blinders on.

"I have not met this Jonah myself," her mom said. "But Sohel spoke very highly of him. And you also are a very good judge of character. If you like him this much, then I expect he also has broken some mold and is very special. Maybe it's possible he is the right kind of man for you?"

"Excuse me."

Kalpani's head shot up and she found Meenu standing in the doorway with her oldest child tucked against her legs. Quickly, Kalpani stood, scanning Meenu and the child for any signs of ill treatment.

"It's okay," Meenu said. "He has a cold only, according to your father." She'd fallen into the speech pattern of the elder generation just in talking to her father. Kalpani breathed easier.

Meenu greeted Kalpani's mother, who offered her some tea, then rose to reheat the water.

"Where are your other little ones?" Kalpani asked, concerned that she had left them with her husband.

"With my mother." Meenu looked Kalpani directly in the eyes for the first time in a long time. "The kids and I are living with my parents now."

Kalpani's throat closed and she fought tears once more. Chetana spun around, one hand to her heart.

Meenu slid into a chair, almost as if her knees had given out at the admission. She and Kalpani grasped hands and squeezed. Kalpani was too choked up to speak.

"We will talk about that sometime in the future," Meenu said, a solemnness in her voice. Then she offered a hesitant smile. "I didn't mean to eavesdrop. But you have never shied away from telling me truths I did not want to hear. It's time now for you to listen to me."

Kalpani grimaced.

"Auntie Chetana is right. If you are considering this man, then he must be very special indeed."

Kalpani raised an eyebrow. She was torn here. Meenu, of all people, advocating commitment after what she'd been through? And yet Meenu knew her well and loved her. It would be wrong not to listen.

"And I think," Meenu said, and smiled in thanks for the tea her mother set in front of her, "that you have taken to heart my situation when you shouldn't have. Others, too, of course." She held Kalpani's gaze.

Kalpani knew she thought of the red-eyed woman who had come to her father for care so many years ago. They had discussed it many times as children but would not now in front of her mother.

"I must be truthful with you now." Meenu took a deep breath. "There were signs. I didn't see them." She shook her head. "No—I chose not to."

Kalpani sucked in a breath, and a shiver traveled down her arms.

"That's me," Meenu said. "It's not you. It will never be you." She reached out to squeeze Kalpani's hand again. "Please do not limit your life or give up a chance at a good man's love because of me. I couldn't bear it."

20

"N*ice.*" Disgusted with himself, Jonah threw his phone on the guest bed at his mom's. Besides averting another run-in with the police, he had known better than to hope for anything more out of texting Kalpani.

Still the one-word response—*Okay*, along with the passcode to Xanadu—annoyed the shit out of him. The code didn't mean she trusted him. She could and would change the numbers as soon as he was gone. And her reticence, sadly, didn't surprise him. She hadn't responded after the wedding weekend, either. Avoidance was, apparently, her MO.

He didn't like it, but honestly, at this point it was probably better this way. He needed to stop liking anything about Kalpani—and fast. The last few days had been brutal.

He'd truly thought he'd met "the one" and that they'd been on some path to happily ever after. That maybe, just maybe, that crazy little Pennsylvania town of True Springs had something with its magical water. Naive, unrealistic thoughts that pegged him as a total sap. He owned it, though. She'd fooled him but good.

Yet the fault was his own. Because from the beginning, she had warned him of two things. One, she never wanted a relationship. And two, she didn't want a messy extraction.

Well, despite the last few weeks of bliss tricking him into believing otherwise, Kalpani had gotten exactly what she'd wanted. He'd walked away, effectively breaking them up, and now he was removing his things from her space, without involving her more than a thirty-second text exchange. No relationship, no drama.

She was probably relieved. She'd had her fun, and now she could dust off her hands and be rid of him just that easy. But he was crushed, bitter, raw, and reeling. Jonah swore for the thousandth time.

Sunday morning, Jonah was still rolling it all around in his head, torturing himself, like the spinning wheel on his computer stuck in its processing loop. Maybe after today —when he could focus on setting up his new studio—he'd be able to start putting it behind him.

He drank a cup of coffee, trying not to wake his mom. But she came out and joined him, concern on her face. She knew perfectly well it wasn't the early hour that was responsible for his misery. "You sure you don't want to try to talk to her?"

"I'm sure."

She pressed her lips together and nodded. "You boys come to the diner for dinner when you're done."

He nodded and left to go pick up the rental van, calling Jake on the way.

"I'm up, I'm up," Jake muttered.

Sadie murmured something awfully close to the phone, and Jonah hung up before he heard anything he didn't want to.

Jeremy was next and answered on the fifth ring. "I'm busy," he said gruffly in lieu of a greeting. Darcy's "you sure are" was audible before the line went dead.

*Shit.* He didn't begrudge his brothers their happiness, or their sex lives, but damn if he needed to feel any worse about his suddenly single status right now.

In a total funk, he retrieved the rental van, then stopped to pick up some sandwiches. Even if they'd already eaten, Jonah suspected they'd need the sustenance long before they called it a day and headed for The Wanderlust. Hauling that wide-format printer up the stairs had been hell. This time they also had to deal with his oversized work table and get both out without marking the freshly painted walls, into the truck, and then into his newly rented studio.

Jonah backed the truck into the small lot behind Xanadu taking up all the parking spaces.

He didn't feel comfortable hanging out inside Xanadu any more than necessary. So, he sat on the low, cold cement stoop, killing time as he waited for his brothers.

He was lucky they were always willing to come to his aid, even on a Sunday when they should be chilling in bed with their soul-mate wives. He hoped they knew he'd do the same for them, but so far, they'd never asked.

He scuffed his boot in the dirt, then leaned back on his elbows to look at the sky. It was gray, like his mood, and he couldn't shake the train of thought.

He was the baby of the family, the fuck-up, the underachiever. If felt like no one had ever counted on him for anything…until Sohel. That, more than anything else, Jonah knew, was the reason that he had never moved on from the print shop. Sohel had appreciated him, needed him, and relied on him—and seemingly never even considered that he shouldn't.

Jonah was kind, thoughtful, conscientious, responsible, and steady. Hell, those were some of his best qualities. He'd proved himself over and over—just by being himself. He was a solid guy—he could be counted on. He wanted to be that for someone—needed to have someone need him.

But Kalpani wasn't ever going to fill that role. She didn't trust easily. She didn't even want commitment, let alone to rely on him—a guy she, for some reason, didn't think that highly of. Even though, he'd thought, he'd proven both his character and his devotion to her.

He shook his head. He wasn't going to settle for that…

But he did need to figure out how to get past it.

Jake and Jeremy strolled up then, and Jonah thanked them for coming.

"Dude, of course," Jeremy said.

"How are you doing?" Jake asked.

They'd known that he and Kalpani had become an item, and he'd considered just letting them continue to think that at least through today. Instead, he told them the shit news when he'd asked them to come and help. Ripping off that Band-Aid quickly was, he figured, another step toward dealing with this new reality.

He shrugged. "Sucks, but whatever."

"There's other fish in the ocean for sure," Jake said.

"Yeah," Jeremy said, "if she doesn't want you, she's crazy." Suddenly, his eyes bugged out.

Jonah heard footsteps on the cinders behind him—then Kalpani's voice. "She's not crazy."

He whipped around.

"And she does want you," Kalpani said.

Jonah's heartbeat hit double time, but his brain stalled. Inexplicably, Kalpani was here, looking nervous, unsure, red-nosed, and puffy-eyed. She clutched a big container of something—her mother's Sunday cooking, from the scent —like a lifeline.

She had just admitted out loud—in front of his brothers —that she wanted him.

He felt a shove from behind, and Jake said, "Say something."

"Hi," he managed, and heard Jeremy groan.

He whirled around to glare at them. "Take a hike. But don't go far. We have work to do."

**21**

---

Kalpani let Jonah's brothers into the salon, their hands laden with food, then breathed a sigh of relief when the door closed behind them. "I didn't expect to be apologizing with an audience."

Jonah's jaw clenched. "You haven't apologized."

"You're right, I haven't." She looked up at him. "I'm sorry." She took a fortifying breath. "So very sorry for assuming the worst, for expecting you to…" She shook her head. "I don't even know what I expected. But I do know I didn't give you a real chance. I didn't judge you on you. I judged you on some preconceived ideas I had. You were right about that, too."

Jonah nodded and his expression softened a little, which made the little glimmer of hope she had flare to life.

"Will you sit?" she asked.

They sat side by side on the cement stoop. She looked at the ground, then at Jonah, her hands unconsciously smoothing over one another. She wanted her comforting lotion—as if it'd protect her—but realized that would only be stalling. She tucked her hands into her armpits. "I'd like to explain."

Kalpani started at the beginning. She talked about the woman with the red eye, and the stylists coming out of the salon with their wads of cash, and her vow to become independent.

She even told him about Meenu. "I planned her shower. I was her maid of honor. I thought I had gotten to know her fiancé well. During those months, I allowed myself to think it was possible to marry for love as a modern Indian woman, with an education and a career, and escape all the traps. He had me snowed, too. I never saw it coming. And then I didn't trust even my own judgment."

"The vow you made as a child cemented itself."

"Yes." She nodded.

"What about your own parents?" Jonah asked.

"My father would never raise a hand to my mother or anyone. He's a gentle, intellectual sort. He's a doctor—not officially, though—and believes in healing people, never harming. But their marriage is more of a 1950s union than what I see in your family."

She looked at the sky and saw a peek of sun through the gray. "Your brothers, and even what I've heard about your parents makes me think that maybe…" She shook her head. "They do seem to prove that it's possible, but it's *you* that matters. You are a good man. The best kind of man. Honorable and thoughtful and giving." She choked back tears. She'd wronged him terribly. "If you are willing to give me another chance…"

Jonah looked at her. "You know I would never hit you or abuse you or—"

"I know," she said. "I never once thought you would."

She shifted to face him better and cleared her throat. "It wasn't ever about that. It's about how easy it is to end up under someone's thumb. Between the Indian marriages I see—so many women subservient to their husbands and dependent on them. And the immigrant experience—almost always on the bottom of the heap, scrabbling, scraping... I promised myself I would never be dependent on anyone but myself, never have to rely on anyone but myself, never be beholden, never let anyone hold me down. Not my father. Not a husband. I promised myself I would *never* marry."

"Ho-whoa," Jonah said. "Okay, I get it. But first of all —I *want* what my parents had. Not the piece of paper, but a true partnership. Equal and supportive. Second, I'm simply not that guy. I'm never going to hamper you. I would be—Jesus—so fucking honored to support you in whatever you want."

Kalpani couldn't hold the tears back any longer. She'd never been the emotional sort, but falling in love with Jonah—yes, dang it, love—and then separating from him had put her through the wringer. "I've never been a crier, but lately..."

Jonah wiped her face with his thumb. "Here's the thing," he said. "You want a whole chain of salons, I'll support you. You're tired of owning your own business and you want to go on a soul-searching trip to India for six weeks? Go. I'll water your plants and adopt your dog and pay your rent."

"I don't have a dog."

"Not yet," he said, and she knew he was teasing her just a bit. "You want me to come with you? I'll carry your bags and keep you safe from creepy men."

"Okay," she said, with a sniff and a smile.

"Wait," Jonah said. "You need to know that someday I would love kids. But I can live without officially getting married."

She nodded. That was actually good. She'd wondered how she would manage kids without a man. Oh, she knew how the science could work, but raising kids alone wasn't that simple.

But Jonah wasn't finished. "You want to make sure I can never own half of your salon, or you'll never be forced to file taxes jointly? Fine. You want to live in sin and tick off your parents, I can deal." He tucked the hair that was sticking to her wet cheeks behind her ears. "As long as I know that you are committed, in this relationship, with me, for keeps, it's all good." He smiled just a little then. "Someday, you change your mind and want to get married? I'm in for that, too."

She sucked in a shaky breath.

His smile slipped, his expression intense now, as he looked into her eyes. "I'm yours, whatever that's going to mean. I just can't do it halfway."

Jonah, as always, seemed to know exactly what she needed. Not a traditional proposal, but a soul-deep, permanent offer of his generous heart and his strong hand.

Hers, forever, if she was brave enough to reach out and grasp it.

Kalpani gulped, tried to speak, and gulped again. Finally, she said, "Yes. I don't want to do it alone after all. I want to do life with you."

Then she just broke down and sobbed with overwhelming relief. She hadn't lost Jonah.

He gathered her into his chest. He was so warm,

strong, and solid. She breathed deep lungfuls of the scent that was his alone—cinnamon and male strength—and slowly, she calmed.

For so long, she'd fought against needing anyone. She never knew how wonderful it could be to have someone you could count on. Someone in it with you, standing tall beside you, navigating every sharp turn and steep hill with their steps matched to yours. And Jonah, she knew now, would be—every step of the way.

**22**

---

*The Wanderlust*
*Sunday, April 19th*

### Rita

Easter had passed. The *second* Easter without Chuck. How was it possible that a whole year had come and gone since he'd died?

And now another Sunday marked her calendar. Rita puttered around the Wanderlust, tidying tables after the lunch crowd had dispersed. They were fully staffed today, and Jake and Sadie were in the kitchen. And in a few hours, Jeremy and Darcy, as well as Jonah and his girl-friend Kalpani, would arrive for an early dinner.

Rita wished Chuck could be there. He would have loved seeing his boys with these fine young women. He had already been proud of the men his sons had become—but seeing them committed and content? That was a whole 'nother ball of wax.

It didn't matter one bit that Jonah and Kalpani claimed they weren't sure they'd ever make it official. Those two were a true love match if Rita had ever seen one. They'd make it.

She had no doubt they'd be successful in their careers, as well. Xanadu was already thriving. And Rita got such a thrill every time she saw the two huge JW canvases hung permanently in each of the front windows. Her son was incredibly talented. Apparently, the women who frequented the salon agreed; they were buying up Jonah's smaller display pieces like hotcakes. Kalpani had tried to coax him back to the salon's top floor, but Jonah had refused to give up the new studio space. Given the stunning work he'd been turning out, Rita thought having a place of his own must be good for his creativity. Then again, she chuckled, maybe it was just Kalpani that was good for him.

Their boys were happy. And they barely needed her. She was thrilled for them and excited to grow the Walker family, truly, but she also felt like a baby bird getting nudged ever so steadily out of her nest.

She knew it was time now to focus on her. She'd grieved—oh yes, she had definitely grieved—but she hadn't moved forward or made any changes. She'd even set her travel dates as far out as possible. The kids had given her the world trip last Mother's Day, for goodness' sake.

She moved to the next table, aligning condiments and double-checking that the seats hadn't any crumbs. When she straightened, she found herself facing the wall of photos and postcards her clients, family, and friends had sent over the years from their vacations and adventures.

Her own adventure was coming up fast. No more excuses; it was time for this old bird to try flapping her wings. Quite frankly, she was both elated and terrified.

The diner had been part of her life even longer than her children had. It was also a strong tie to her husband. Frustrated, she tossed the rag she'd been using on the table. Dammit, she still missed Chuck so much. But Jake and Sadie were perfectly capable of running the place. It was time she let them.

She'd been feeling awkward about coming back after her six-week journey around the world. Did she just reinsert herself? What else did she even know how to do? Where else would she go?

No way could she sit home in her empty house—Chuck gone, Jonah officially moving out soon to live in a new place with Kalpani—and do nothing but twiddle her thumbs. She didn't even know how to knit, and it had been ages since she'd bowled. She barely watched television. She'd simply never gotten in the habit, because she'd never had time.

Before she could get herself too worked up, she took a deep breath, and then one more. She pulled her cell phone from her apron pocket and called her sister.

Reenie answered on the first ring. "I was just about to call you. I'm going to the mall. Bathing suit shopping. The Riviera calls for a new one, don't you think?" Reenie was to be Rita's travel companion on the world tour. The boys hadn't wanted her to go alone, felt it wasn't safe, and Rita was just fine with that. Although Reenie at times would surely try her patience, they'd have a lot of laughs.

Rita laughed. "Lord, I guess that means I have to try some on, too." No woman should ever buy a swimsuit without a second opinion, and she and her sister had eliminated a lot of near disasters by teaming up in the past.

"I'll pick you up. I can be there in fifteen."

"We'll have to shop fast. I want to be back for dinner with the kids."

"No problem."

"Hang on," Rita said, "I wanted to run something by you."

"What's that?"

Seeing their sister Ruby at Jeremy's wedding had given Rita an idea. "What would you think if we added on to our trip?"

"Like how? And don't suggest the Great Wall of China or Mount Everest. These old hips can't handle it."

"You think those hips could handle a horse?"

"A horse?" Reenie screeched. Rita heard the laugh in her voice, though.

She pulled a postcard from the wall. It was faded and curled, but the mountains were still gorgeous.

"Yes. I'm thinking if Billy Crystal can handle it, so can we. And Ruby did say those Montana ranch hands are the best view around."

———

Thank you for reading *Dreaming of Forever with You*! I hope you enjoyed it and want a little more Rita. She's not quite ready yet for act two (it's coming!), but she's got cameos alongside a new cast of characters in the next *Love That Lasts* book: *Starting Over Together*.

When widow Caroline finds a new beginning on a

Montana ranch, she's shocked to discover she's ready to give love a second chance. Sam has promised himself never to let a woman come between him and what's important again. What will it take to convince this cowboy that true love is worth the risk ?

Go get *Starting Over Together* now,
or turn the page for the SNEAK PEAK!

# STARTING OVER TOGETHER

"You are going to True Springs for me, Caroline Murphy, and you are not to come back home until you've taken a thousand—no, two thousand—photographs!" Neve held up two fingers right in front of Caroline's face.

Caroline lifted her palms up in supplication. An immediate queasiness gripped her gut, but no words would form.

Her best friend wasn't waiting for an answer anyway. Neve Hoffman had already begun tearing through Caroline's closet, her Lycra-covered rear wiggling in the doorway.

Just before this outburst, Neve had asked—insisted, really—that Caroline drive from Miami to Pennsylvania to deliver an engagement ring to Neve's ex-husband's family for her. Apparently dear Grandpa was old school and didn't trust a tracking number from the United States Post Office, UPS, or even FedEx. Not with this ring, anyway. And Neve had a jammed schedule and a full life, while Caroline had, well, nothing.

Caroline shook her head and forced her jaw to move. "How did we get from personalized ring delivery to filling some scenic scrapbook?"

No response. Instead, her determined friend wrestled some luggage out of the closet and threw all of it onto the unmade bed. Two large duffel bags and Caroline's biggest suitcase. Not a weekend jaunt. Where in the world was this True Springs, and just how long did Neve expect her to stay?

As her friend fished for the zipper on the oversized roller board, Caroline turned away. She crossed to the high his-and-hers dresser, resting her chin on her hands before a framed photograph of her husband. Kevin looked handsome, proud, and a little uptight, buttoned to his chin in his starched police officer's uniform. Caroline traced a finger over his face. Her own reflection hovered on the dusty glass.

*Zip, zip, zip.* The suitcase had been opened. Caroline registered the noise, but she didn't turn to watch. Here on the dresser, with a trick of the light, she could see herself with Kevin again. She pretended that they were about to enter their fourth year of marriage, content and happy, and were ready to start a family. Perhaps their first baby would arrive near her own thirtieth birthday.

"Caroline, I need to get into those drawers." Neve pulled at her waist, shattering Caroline's optical illusion and impossible fantasy. She slid her hands from the dresser, sighed, and straightened.

Neve wagged her finger again.

"I get why you *need* me to be your errand girl," Caroline said. Neve's days were booked solid as a working, single mom, her daughter Bella was in school, and Caroline was doing nothing—not working, not socializing, not exercising, not shopping or cleaning, or taking care of herself very well. "But can't we just pay someone? There are people who deliver cars. Surely there are people who deliver rings."

"It has to be you."

"I don't want to leave." She'd barely left home in two years, and she certainly wasn't going to start now, just because Neve said so.

"Oh, I know. But you have to get out of this—this *shrine*." Neve's face twisted with disgust. "You need to connect with people again."

"I do. I—"

Neve planted her hands on her hips and pursed her lips. "Other than me, Bella, and Noreen."

Bella was Neve's seven-year-old daughter, and one of the only bright spots in Caroline's lame existence. Noreen was Neve's mother and— Caroline shuddered.

Neve rubbed Caroline's upper arms over her grungy, shapeless t-shirt. "Honey, you aren't grieving for Kevin anymore. You've just given up on you. It's been nearly two years."

Caroline felt nearly mesmerized by Neve's soothing voice and the friction of her hands.

"Instead of moving forward, you're falling apart." Neve stopped rubbing, and her focus shifted to Caroline's face. "Enormous dark circles have nearly swallowed up your gorgeous eyes. Your cheeks are hollow—I can practically see your bones."

"The Grief Diet," Caroline said. "Works wonders. Wouldn't recommend it to just anyone, though."

Neve shook her head and cupped her hands around

Caroline's face. "I'm certain it's against Florida law for a person to parade around this pale."

"You sure know how to make a girl feel good," Caroline said without any heat.

"I'm trying to make you see what I see."

Caroline wrenched her chin away. "You think I don't know?" She rubbed her forehead with her fingers. "I just…"

She shrugged, giving up on words, but her heart whispered, *I just…can't… I'm lost… I'm scared…*

*Damn.* Here was her best friend, trying to help, no matter how misguided. "You're a good mom, Neve. I mean, not just to Bella, but to me, too."

"I'd rather just be your friend, but you need more than that now." Neve wrapped her in a fierce hug, then stepped away and looked her in the eye. "You need someone who's willing to push. I never should have waited this long to do it."

"I don't want to leave. Kevin's here, in our home." Tears welled in Caroline's eyes. "I miss him so much."

"Oh, sweetie. You'll miss him forever." Neve smoothed Caroline's lank hair away from her face. "But you can't stop living to keep his memory alive. You have to start shooting pictures—"

Caroline shook her head.

"You don't have to go back to the *Herald*. But you always found joy in using your camera."

Neve's tone had been gentle, but Caroline's reaction was vehement. "Not anymore. I'm not touching the thing."

"I can't see what photography has to do with Kevin's death. You were on vacation."

"Best friend or no, this topic is none of your business."

Caroline's tone was harsh. She'd told Neve this over and over.

Neve pressed her lips together. "That hurts."

"Yeah, well, if you keep pressing me, you're gonna hurt a whole lot worse." Caroline avoided Neve's direct gaze and moved to sit on her unmade bed. The only reason the sheets were clean was because Neve's mother, Noreen, invaded every Tuesday like clockwork. All day long. Cleaning and washing and talking. And talking and talking. Loudly. Incessantly. And worst of all, she insisted on answers. Noreen thought conversation was "healthy" for Caroline and was determined to fit a week's worth into every visit. She wouldn't stop coming, no matter what Caroline said or did. Tuesdays equaled torture.

Neve raised her chin. "You leave me no choice. Hardball it is."

"You can't make me."

"Oh, but I can." Neve's eyes held a wicked glint, her smile a smug twist. "Noreen's waiting for my call. She's prepared to move in at a moment's notice."

Caroline gasped. "You wouldn't dare."

"I would, and so would she. In fact, Noreen has grown tired of seeing you waste your life." Neve tilted her head and admired her manicure. "And what's more, she believes you'll never get back on your feet if you don't gain fifteen pounds, have live-in companionship, involve yourself with a worthwhile charity—to remind you that you are not alone in sorrow—and"—Neve paused to look her in the eye—"discard ninety percent of Kevin's possessions."

Caroline's hands flew to her mouth. "She said that?"

"Word for word. Remember when she ransacked my place?" Neve grimaced. "Rand had to buy out Goodwill to get his things back, right down to his hair gel. And then she browbeat my attorney until he waived all his fees—a bribe to call her off."

Caroline had rather thought Neve's ex deserved all that and more, but… "I'm not her daughter."

"Ever since your mom died, she's considered you her daughter, too." Neve's mouth set in a grim line.

Caroline stared in horror. "You're dead set on this, aren't you?"

"One ring. Two thousand photographs." Neve didn't even crack a smile. "Are you packing, or am I?"

Triage nurse turned physical therapist—Neve Hoffman was skilled at bulldozing any patient who told her no. Her mother Noreen, on the other hand, operated more like King Kong: terrifying and destructive despite essential goodness underneath.

Caroline knew better than to stand in the duo's path while in a weakened condition. She flopped back onto the bed and pulled a pillow over her face. "You pack."

"I was hoping you'd say that," Neve said.

Caroline heard a drawer slide out as her friend murmured to herself, "Early September in True Springs. Should still be warm. Shorts. Tanks. Cropped leggings. Push-up bras are a must. Thongs definitely…"

Read *Starting Over Together* next!

*Love That Lasts* series:

Faking It Together (#1)
Second Chance Love Affair (#2)
Dreaming of Forever with You (#3)
Starting Over Together (#4)
*and*
Making Forever with You (Prequel
—*co-authored with Savannah Kade!*)

# THANKS AND MORE

I'm so thrilled you found *Dreaming of Forever with You*! Would you kindly share your enjoyment of the story by leaving a brief review on Goodreads, BookBub, or your retailer? Reviews and word of mouth (*please do tell a friend!*) are still the best way for readers to find books they'll love. So grateful for each and every review —thank you!

I love to hear from readers, and these days there are so many ways for us to connect! On my website (www. jbschroederauthor.com), you can subscribe to my newsletter to have news delivered right to your email inbox or visit the Finding JB page to reach me via my social media links—choose what works for you. If you prefer *only* new release alerts, however, simply follow me on BookBub or Amazon.

# ACKNOWLEDGMENTS

Although authors exist happily in our own heads and frequently buddy up to our keyboards for companionship, we most certainly do not write alone.

Thank you to Christi Snow, Savannah Kade, and Eli Collier for so graciously lending their wisdom and excellent instincts to a draft that was an even rougher slog than usual.

Amber Leechalk, thank you for lending your expertise to make my story work. So glad you went to law school, my little chicken woofer!

Arran McNichol, the fastest copyeditor in the states, how is it possible you impress me more every time?

Jen Coleman, proofreader extraordinaire, I am so glad to know you. Thank you for your eagle eyes and your spot-on suggestions!

There are not words to express how grateful I am to my JB's Review Crew—always ready, always kind, always amazing! You release a load of worry off my shoulders and bring huge smiles to my face!

Femmes, my old friends: Thank you for answering my call for help to give this book an extra leg up! Can't tell you how much I appreciate it.

MK Quinn: so pleased you reached out! Thank you for the lovely quote. *Let's stick together…yeah-yeah-yeah*!

A rafters-style shout out to my immediate family, who was locked-down with me from the middle of *Dreaming of Forever with You*'s rough draft right on through release. Thanking my lucky stars that I like you (still) and you get me and my dreams. Love you all.

And to all my readers, thank you, thank you, thank you, a million times and counting.

# ABOUT THE AUTHOR

JB SCHROEDER, a graduate of Penn State University's creative writing program, writes both contemporary romance and romantic suspense—in other words: *romance to make your heart race*. She adores stories about everyday people embracing new beginnings—especially when the characters need a little help from true love.

www.jbschroederauthor.com